KAY D. RIZZO

The Prodigal Daughter
A True Story

Pacific Press®
Publishing Association

Nampa, Idaho | Oshawa, Ontario, Canada
www.pacificpress.com

Cover design by Gerald Lee Monks
Cover design resources from iStockphoto.com and Dreamstime.com
Inside design by Kristin Hansen-Mellish

The author assumes full responsibility for the accuracy of all facts and quotations as cited in this book.

Unless otherwise noted, Scripture quotations are from the HOLY BIBLE, NEW INTERNATIONAL VERSION®, NIV®. Copyright © 1973, 1978, 1984, 2011 by Biblica, Inc.® Used by permission. All rights reserved worldwide.

You can obtain additional copies of this book by calling toll-free 1-800-765-6955 or by visiting http://www.adventistbookcenter.com.

Library of Congress Cataloging-in-Publication Data:

Rizzo, Kay D., 1943-
  The prodigal daughter : a true story / by Kay D. Rizzo.
     pages cm
  ISBN 13: 978-0-8163-5420-7 (pbk.)
  ISBN 10: 0-8163-5420-0 (pbk.)
1. Young women. 2. Human trafficking. 3. Fathers and daughters. 4. Prodigal son (Parable). 5. Hollywood (Los Angeles, Calif.). I. Title.
  PS3568.I836P76 2014
  813'.54—dc23
                                        2014015978

July 2014

Table of Contents

Introduction

The Prodigal Daughter: A True Story is based on one very real young woman's journey into the sordid underbelly of today's society and then back home again to a father who loves her. Like the parable of the prodigal son, this story speaks more of the heart of a loving father than that of an errant child.

This current-day adaptation of the old, familiar tale Jesus told about how low one young man fell in the eyes of Jewish society and how far the loving father willingly stooped to lift him out of his filth, reminds us of how far our heavenly Father will go to redeem and restore His royal sons and daughters. Refresh the details of the story in your memory by rereading Luke 15:11–32.

When I first heard "the prodigal daughter's" story, I knew it had to be shared. But I worried that the depths to which "Brianna" fell would be too harsh for Christian readers to ingest. Then I realized that I was not rehashing the tawdry tale to benefit the "older sibling" of the family, but for each of us who has, at one time or another, shed her dignity to later be rescued from the resulting debauchery by a forgiving Savior.

Author Francine Rivers's retelling of the romance of Gomer and Hosea in *Redeeming Love* assured me that such a story could be told.

The message of Rivers's book deeply affected the way I "saw" myself in relation to God's acceptance and forgiveness.

Engrossed in the life of San Francisco's 1850s, I quickly forgot I was reading a parable. So when the prostitute ran away from her forgiving husband for the third time, I mentally slammed shut the book and thought, *How unrealistic! No woman in her right mind would abandon the love and security of a caring spouse and return to the seamy life of a streetwalker!*

And *Pow!* Reality struck. The Holy Spirit blindsided me with the truth. *"Kay, that's what you do every time you return to your old sins!"*

I am praying that as you read *The Prodigal Daughter,* you will keep your mind and your Bible open to Jeremiah 33:3. And by the time you finish reading the last phrase of the book, you will have a renewed appreciation for the prayers of faithful parents, the forgiveness our Savior bestows on His wayward children, and the eternal love He lavishes on each of us daily.

A note to the reader: The names, locations, and several details of the story have been altered to protect the privacy of those involved.

CHAPTER ONE

In the Beginning

Where does Brianna's story truly begin? After the final curtain call at the summer production of *Beauty and the Beast*? Or when a Hollywood talent scout handed the nineteen-year-old his business card, inviting her to "look him up" if she ever found herself in Hollywood?

Perhaps the deciding moment came on the sultry afternoon in August when then nine-year-old Brianna; her stoic, older sister, Elizabeth; and their father stood at the graveside of his wife and their mother. Whenever Bob closed his eyes, he could feel the child's death grip about his waist, her face buried in his chest. Was the beginning of the tale when Brianna took her first independent baby steps? Or did this narrative actually start when his newborn daughter wrapped her tiny fist around his pinkie finger and he felt loath to ever let her go?

Outside Bob Austin III's office door, a wall clock gonged three times. The man rubbed his tired eyes. He had a ton of paperwork to do before the morning. He'd tried to sleep earlier, but after hearing the family heirloom announce midnight, one, and then two, he gave up and returned to the familiar comfort of his oak-paneled office. Once there, he paced back and forth in front of the floor-to-ceiling glass-paned window and fretted. During the day, the window looked out on his first orange grove. At night, it looked out on total darkness.

Where is my Honey Bee? he wondered. He and his wife had dubbed Brianna, their younger daughter, "Honey Bee" due to her insatiable appetite for giving and receiving affection. *Was it so long ago that she eagerly ran into my arms whenever I returned from the orchards? When was the last time she hopped into my lap and begged me to "scratch" her back— her term for a massage? When did the Hershey's Kisses hidden in the drawers of my desk disappear and the love "stickers" of cats, puppies, and butterflies stop appearing in my luggage when I made overnight trips out of town?*

Don't misunderstand. While Brianna brought sunshine into his life, his older daughter Elizabeth brought order out of chaos. "What a treasure," he told his colleagues. She was the son he'd never had. Even as a toddler, Elizabeth had been nicknamed "Busy Bee" by her mother. Daughter number one had always been conscientious and industrious, almost to a fault. Elizabeth stuck to an assigned task until it was done to her liking—not merely to her father's liking, but to hers.

On the day Bob's wife died after a long battle with pancreatic cancer, fifteen-year-old Elizabeth stepped into the role of what she called "chief cook and bottle washer." She cared for the home, kept the meals coming, and saw to it that her younger sister was dressed and on time for school each morning. When the girl threatened to put off attending college, Bob hired Maude to run the home and make the meals.

Elizabeth completed her accounting degree in record time and immediately took over the books for the 3 B's Orchards with her usual aplomb. When Bob accepted the appointment of acting regional director for the California Citrus Growers' Association, she virtually ran the day-by-day business at 3 B's Orchards. Even Ken Raab, the business field manager and her eventual choice of a husband, fit perfectly into the organization like the missing piece of the family's jigsaw puzzle.

Bob glanced at the oval-framed, sepia photo hanging above the fireplace. The stoic face of his grandfather—the original owner of 3 B's Orchards, which he named for his three sons—looked down at Bob. The somber frown on his face didn't do justice to the old man's wry sense of humor and contagious zest for life. He willed the business to Bob III after his son Bob died in the Korean War; Bob Jr.'s younger brother Bill died in a hunting accident; and Ben, his youngest son, moved to New

York City to pursue a career on Wall Street. Bob III and his wife, Angela, continued the company tradition by naming their daughters Elizabeth, or "Bette," and Brianna, or "Bri." And he rounded out the trio of Bs for the 3 B's Orchards.

The salty-haired man shook his head and lowered his two-hundred-pound frame into his aging, high-backed, cowhide leather office chair and swiveled around toward his computer screen. *What's happening in the world tonight?* he mused as he brought up a recap of the evening news from CNN.

His gaze rested on the silver framed photo of his wife, Angie. There was no escaping the fact that Bette had inherited her mother's head for organization, while Brianna displayed her mother's beguiling smile and quick wit. He harbored a bittersweet blend of joy and concern. He loved his older daughter with all his heart but Bri's and his had always been a different kind of love story, not the traditional boy meets girl romance, of course, but a love between a sometimes-indulgent father and his willful, capricious daughter.

CHAPTER TWO

A New Star in the Heavens

Enthusiastic whistles and thunderous applause echoed off the plastered walls of the small community theater, demanding a fourth curtain call for the cast of *Beauty and the Beast*. The musical's six-week run had ended with a triumphant performance. Again, the curtains parted, the acting troupe took their well-deserved bows, and the curtains closed.

As the actors broke out of formation, Simon, Bri's leading man, kissed her cheek. "Great job tonight, Bri."

"Thanks, Simon. You too."

His hand lingered on her shoulder a little longer than usual. "Coming to the cast party at De Casa's?"

She flashed him a flirty smile. "Of course. I wouldn't miss it for the world." The laughing leading lady swirled across the stage, almost falling into the arms of a balding, middle-aged stranger.

"Splendid performance as Belle, Miss Austin. Splendid indeed!" The stranger thrust a business card into her hand. "I believe you have genuine star quality. If you ever decide to pursue an acting career in Hollywood, give me a call."

Before she could respond, the stranger strolled stage left and exited the building. The nineteen-year-old gasped and stared at the gold lettering on the white card: "Maxwell Talent Agency—Clyde Maxwell, talent scout."

The girl dashed off stage into the waiting arms of Ron Chaney, her best friend and personal bodyguard since third grade. Even Roger Block, the class bully, knew better than to taunt her when Ron was around.

Breathless with excitement, she flipped her long blond curls off her back. "They loved me, didn't they, Ronnie? The audience loved me!"

"Yes, they loved you, Honey Bee. Who wouldn't?" He brushed a stray curl from the side of her heavily made-up cheek. "You delivered a stellar performance!"

"Are you sure? Or are you just saying that?"

"I wouldn't lie to you, sweet love."

"Oh, you're such a dear. What would I do without you?" She stood on tiptoe to kiss his cheek.

A group of newspaper and local television reporters had gathered on center stage. One enthusiastic photojournalist called, "Over here, Miss Austin. Look this way." Several cameras flashed as the blond-haired beauty with the snapping blue eyes blew kisses to her audience. Ron slipped his arm about the girl's slim waist and whispered, "Come on. Let's get out of here."

"You know we can't skip the traditional cast party, Ronnie. What would people think?"

Before he could reply, a graying theater critic from the local TV news station, reeking of cigar smoke, shoved a microphone in Bri's face. "So now that the theater season is over, what are your plans, Miss Austin? College? Broadway?" The engaging TV lothario flashed a come-hither grin.

Bri slipped a strand of hair behind one ear, winked, and emitted a tinkling giggle. "I guess you'll just have to wait to find out, won't you, Mr. Owens?"

Ron leaned closer to Bri's ear and whispered, "Come on, Honey Bee, let's go."

The young woman allowed him to escort her to the female cast members' dressing room door where she paused and pressed her hands against his chest. "Stay, Ron, stay! You know the girls wouldn't appreciate having you burst in on them while they're changing into their street clothes." She giggled.

He gave a jerky nod and stepped aside. "Uh, yes, of course." As she opened the dressing room door, Ron planted a quick kiss on her cheek.

"You are so good to me, Ronnie. We won't stay long at the party. After a slice or two of pizza, we'll leave, I promise."

"I'm holding you to that." His hand lingered on her fingertips until she closed the door behind her.

Less than an hour later, the couple slipped away from the celebrating throng at the town's only pizza joint. "Here. You drive." She tossed Ron her car keys and hopped into the passenger side of her citrus yellow Miata ragtop, her graduation gift from her father. Her seat belt had barely clicked into place when the engine roared to life and their favorite CD filled the night air. She glanced at Ron. *I think he loves this car more than even me,* she mused as the vehicle spun gravel out of the restaurant's parking lot.

A caressing breeze whipped Bri's long blond curls about her face and shoulders. Brushing a pesky lock from her forehead, she threw back her head and sighed with delight. Few pleasures equaled speeding through the warm summer night air to pop singer Kelly Clarkson's hit ballad, "A Moment Like This."

The lights of the little valley town twinkled in the rearview mirror as the sports car wound its way past the citrus groves up to the crest of Arnold's Knoll, a popular parking spot for local teens. Ron eased the Miata into their favorite turnout that overlooked the entire valley. As he turned off the engine, the singer's gentle twang faded, to be replaced by the whisper of wind blowing through the tall grass.

From as far north as the eye could see to the southernmost visible point, the valley spread out like the sweeping train of a diva's black velvet gown sprinkled with glorious clusters of jewels scattered in wild disarray. Bri hopped out of the car, waved her arms in the air, and spun about like a small child, her skirt rippling around her knees. She paused to hug herself. "Have you ever seen anything so beautiful?"

Ron rounded the vehicle and slipped up behind her, drawing her close in his arms. "Never." He brushed her tousled curls to one side and nuzzled her neck. "You are so beautiful."

"Oh, Ron." She laughed and whirled about to face him. "I'm talking about the valley, you Pooh Bear." Bri had nicknamed him Pooh Bear after he had played Winnie the Pooh in their third-grade play, and somehow the nickname stuck.

"You might have been, but I wasn't." He planted a kiss squarely on her lips. As he lifted his face from hers, he whispered, "I've been waiting to do that all evening, especially after that Neanderthal kissed you in the last scene of the play. Every night I've wanted to knock the grin off his drooling face."

Bri giggled. "Oh, Ron, don't be silly. The poor boy didn't mean anything. He was merely acting." Silently, she smiled with pleasure at Ron's macho attitude. She always felt safe with him around to protect her. Resting her head against his chest, she ran one finger between the collar of his denim shirt and his neck. "Remember, when I become a star, I'll play a lot of romantic scenes, but they won't mean anything to me as long as I have you."

"I heard what that talent agent said." He tightened his hold on her and buried his face in her curls. "You're thinking about taking him up on his offer, aren't you?"

"I would love to. You, more than anyone, know an acting career has been my dream since grade school." She ran a light finger around one of his ears. "Hey, if I do, there's no reason you can't come with me, is there? You could become a star too. You made an adorable Pooh Bear. You know my father. He would be beside himself with worry if I were to go alone. But if you went with me . . ." Her words trailed off into a teasing whisper.

"What? Me? Hollywood is your dream, Bri, not mine."

"Tell me you've never thought about an acting career."

"Only as a wild and crazy fantasy; not as a solid career move. Besides, the last time we talked about this, I thought we agreed we'd get two years of college under our belts before making any serious decisions about the future."

"That was before Mr. What's-his-name gave me his card and told me I was good enough for the stage. He told me to look him up. It's important I strike while the iron's hot, don't you think?"

Ron shook his head and sighed.

"It's not like acting is a whim or a new idea, Ronnie. I've talked of little else for years. And I know that with you by my side, I can make it. I can become a star."

He eased her out of his arms. "Are you suggesting I just go along for the ride? I have dreams too, you know."

"Yeah, I know, but I love you, Pooh Bear. You are my muse, my inspiration. I can't do this without you." She clicked her tongue. "And it's not like you can't take classes and become a cop a year or even five years from now; but for an actress, age is everything. I can't put off following my dream until I'm older, not if I'm really serious about it. This agent could be my big break, Ronnie."

He drew her closer. She could feel his voice rumbling in her chest. "You're serious, aren't you?"

"Yes, I think I am." She stepped back and lifted her round, pleading, blue eyes to meet his, knowing the impact of her wishes on him.

Again, he shook his head. "Bri, be reasonable. You and I can't just abandon everything and take off for Hollywood on a whim. What would we live on until we found work? I certainly don't have enough in my savings for police academy tuition to pay the security fee and first month's rent even on a walk-up studio apartment, certainly not in Los Angeles."

She teased a stray curl from off his furrowed brow. "With your rakish good looks, your winning smile, and your sexy black hair, you will break into the acting business in no time. Besides, you were great in our senior class play." She ran her pinkie finger along the dimple in his chin. "Oh Pooh Bear, you've obviously been thinking about it. That's what I love so much about you. I can always depend on you to watch my back." She snuggled closer into his arms.

"Besides, we won't have to drain your savings account for our Hollywood adventure. My grandpa Austin set up a trust fund for me. He was quite wealthy, you know. The Austins owned half of Kings County while my mother's folks owned the other." She laughed. "Technically, I'm not supposed to have access to my trust fund until my twenty-first birthday, but I'm sure I can convince Daddy to get it released a couple of months early."

"More like a couple of years." He pulled free of her arms. "You really believe your oh-so-practical father will agree to such a scheme?"

"Don't worry. I know my dad. Besides, I'm his Honey Bee, remember?" Bri threw back her head and whirled about in abandon. As the cascade of rocks and loose soil she was standing on broke free from the sandstone cliff and tumbled down to the valley below, Ron grabbed her arm and yanked her back from the edge.

"Oh, that was close!" A hysterical laugh escaped from her throat. An adrenaline rush and a heightened sense of danger swept through her.

"Oh, Bri! You scare me sometimes." He drew her close again. "What if I hadn't been here to keep you from falling?"

"That's why I need you so much, you big old Pooh Bear." She again snuggled into his embrace. Feeling his arms wrapped around her and his steady heartbeat throbbing in her ear gave her the reassurance she needed to convince him of the urgency of her plan. *He might have worries and concerns at this moment, but when I'm a star on TV or the lead in my first film, he'll realize he made the right choice,* she reasoned. *Then, if he still insists on playing cops and robbers by attending his little police academy, I'll be able to help him financially. One thing is certain, I don't want to end up like "little Miss Perfect"!*

Big sister Bette always colored within the lines. She graduated from high school in three years and from college with high honors. She predictably married the boy next door and stepped into the family business without missing a beat. To Bri, her sister seemed born to run 3 B's Orchards. The younger girl wrinkled her nose at the thought. *All that is missing from Bette's life is a passel of runny-nosed kids hanging on to her grubby blue jeans.* It wasn't that Bri didn't like children; she did, as long as they were someone else's. Besides, she had time enough to ruin her slim waistline with a pregnancy or two.

Bette seemed middle-aged, a stodgy, pony-tailed hausfrau years before her time. *It's like she skipped over her teenage years into a predictable adult pattern. That's not going to happen to me! No way! I want to really live my life. I want to taste, feel, and experience everything—not vegetate into a routine of day-to-day boredom in my father's orange groves.*

Setting her jaw, she vowed to herself, *I'll make it big. Even Daddy will be proud of me.* Her face softened at the thought of her patient, caring father. Like Ron, he'd always been there for her, supporting her every endeavor, always her biggest cheerleader. That he could be overprotective at times occasionally rankled her, but all in all, she knew she could count on him. A satisfied smile teased her lips as she imagined seeing his beaming face in the midst of the celebrating crowd at the Oscars. She would publically thank him for his undying support and love.

Ron broke into her dreamy reverie. "We should be heading back. Your dad will be worried."

"What time is it, anyway?"

"I don't know, but the first rays of sunlight are peeking over the Sierras. Perhaps you should give him a call on your cell phone."

"What, and waken him? Trust me; that would not be cool!" Her laughter filled the early morning air.

CHAPTER THREE

Memories

The Miller clock, an heirloom his wife's family brought west in a dilapidated, mule-drawn Conestoga wagon four generations earlier, gonged five times. Bob Austin started awake. He'd developed a kink in his neck while napping in his office chair. Wrenching his neck from side to side, he ran his fingers through his thick salt-and-pepper mane.

It's 5:00 A.M. Where is Bri? That little minx knows I worry about her when she stays out so late. She should have called. The craggy-faced fifty-year-old, owner of the 3 B's Orchards, glanced at the silver filigree framed photo on the edge of his desk and sighed. "That girl is gonna be the death of me yet, Angie, love."

The silver and bronze frame beside his wife's photo held four smiling faces gathered around the base of a Christmas tree. It was a reminder of a happier time, a time when Angela, the love of his life, welcomed him home from the groves with the aroma of homemade stew bubbling on the stove or a batch of oatmeal-raisin cookies fresh from the oven, and a heart-melting kiss, always a kiss.

A smile teased the corners of his lips as he recalled a time when his two bright-eyed daughters would run into his arms, eager to share their day's adventures with him. Grabbing a daughter under each of his arms, he twirled them about as they giggled and squealed with delight. He inhaled slowly and then exhaled sharply. "Snap out of it, old boy. Those days are forever gone!"

In the ten years since Angie's death, the girls had grown into lovely young women; lovely, but distant. While twenty-four-year-old Elizabeth, or Bette, as he called his eldest, worked by his side as the chief financial officer of 3 B's Orchards, her heart and attention were turned toward Ken, her wiry-haired, rangy husband and the field supervisor of 3 B's Orchards. *As it should be,* Bob acknowledged to himself. *As it should be.*

The fruit-producing orchards sprawled over several miles of prime river land in Central California's San Joaquin Valley. Growing up, Bob had often heard the story of Grandpa Robert and Grandma Bethany Austin's dust bowl trek from Norman, Oklahoma, to Amarillo, Texas, and then on to California's Central Valley.

Upon arriving in California, the couple, barely out of their teens, moved from farm to farm following the harvest. Cotton pickers, gooseberry grubbers, grape harvesters; lettuce, tomato, almond, and, of course, citrus fruit growers—they did it all. Over the years, they scrimped and did without to buy acreage, all the while struggling to raise two sons. On their undeveloped piece of the valley, they dreamed of planting orange trees "as far as the eye could see."

The Austins' younger son, Lyle, died at Pearl Harbor; Robert, the older boy, and Bob's dad, fulfilled his parents' dream until he became the wealthiest orange grower in the region. When Robert III married Angela Thompson, he inherited the Austin orange groves as well as the extensive Thompson spread.

Bob shook the cobwebs from his brain, steeled his jaw, and attempted to study the current spreadsheet Bette had left on his desk.

An aging air-conditioner unit on the roof above his head waged a valiant battle against the oppressive and enervating temperatures. The heat wave spread from California's southern border north to Oregon's Klamath rain forest. *If these temperatures don't break soon, the heat will damage this year's citrus crop. Too many families will suffer.* He clicked his tongue and sighed.

Shoving his chair back from the desk, he rose to his feet and stretched. Painful kinks in his back reminded him that age was not a rumor, that he was no longer a young buck in his forties. At the sound of the first workers pulling their cars and minivans into the shipping yard, he strode over to the window and watched as several of his hired hands gathered around Ken to receive instructions for the day. At the other end of the house, the kitchen door slammed, announcing his housekeeper's arrival.

"Good morning, Mr. Bob," Maude called from the hallway. "Another hot day out there. Will you be wanting blueberry muffins or corn bread with your eggs this morning?" The seventy-plus woman popped her frosty white head around the office doorjamb. "My goodness! You look a mess. Have you been up all night?"

"Pretty much." He grunted and ran his fingers through his tousled hair. "Just waiting for my little girl to get home."

"Brianna? She must be home. Her car is parked by the kitchen door."

"You're kidding." He strode past his housekeeper to the kitchen door and opened it. The early morning sunlight glinted off the windshield of Bri's citrus yellow Miata convertible.

"See, Mr. Bob. It's there."

He groaned and sighed. "I didn't hear her come in. I guess I got more sleep than I thought." He closed the door and turned toward the staircase. "I need a shower and a shave."

"Your breakfast will be waiting for you when you come down, including a batch of blueberry pancakes . . . or would you prefer the muffins?"

"Either sounds good." He waved his hand absently in the air and started up the stairs.

At the second-floor landing, he passed by his younger daughter's closed bedroom door and resisted the urge to peek in just to be sure. Instead, he knocked. "Bri, Maude is making breakfast. Will you be joining us?"

He thought he heard a sleepy, nondescript voice garble an indecipherable reply. *At least she's safely home.* He smiled, broke into a whistling version of "Stars and Stripes Forever," and hurried to the master bedroom. As he hauled his sweaty T-shirt over his head, he nodded, "Yep, a shower is just what I need!"

Twenty minutes later, the refreshed owner of 3 B's Orchards bounded down the stairs like a young gazelle on the first day of spring. All the memories of terrible imaginings of what might have happened to Bri had faded. His baby girl was home—safe and sound. But could she have called him to tell him she would be late? That's what Bette would have done. But Bri would never be Bette and Bette would never be Bri. As much as he loved each of his daughters for their unique personalities, he had to admit that he sometimes wished they could have blended more; that Bette could be a little more relaxed and Bri a little more thoughtful of others.

"Good morning, Maude. It's a beautiful day, a beautiful—" He stopped midsentence and stared at his younger daughter sitting in her customary chair at the table.

"Good morning, Daddy!" She hopped to her feet and planted a kiss on his cheek. He gaped in surprise.

"Didn't you just answer me from your room when I called?"

She giggled. "Must have heard my radio playing." Bri sat back down and cut off a forkful of pancakes. A swirl of maple syrup and a dollop of whipped cream lingered on her lips. "Miss Maude's blueberry pancakes are heavenly as usual. Wait until you taste 'em. She added pecans. And you know how much I love pecans."

"Good morning to you as well." As he pulled out his chair from the table, the family's long-haired tabby cat rubbed against his legs. "Shoo, Hiram. Go bug Maude." He opened his napkin and placed it on his lap.

"*Thanks,* Mr. Bob. That animal is determined to trip me up this morning. Shoo, cat!" She clapped her hands together. The animal darted for cover under the table.

Bob laughed. His and the housekeeper's conversation began the same way every morning, always with Hiram, but neither would have chosen to live without the furry creature. While Maude poured him a tumbler of freshly squeezed orange juice, he turned toward Bri. "So, what got you up so early, Honey Bee?"

"You, Daddy." She swallowed a gulp of milk and wiped the mustache from her mouth with her sleeve, like a five-year-old.

"OK, let's have it. You are never this chipper in the morning. By the way, what time did you get home last night?"

"Oh, I don't know. I came into your office to kiss you good night but you were sleeping so peacefully, I didn't have the heart to awaken you." Her eyes sparkled.

"I assume you attended the cast party last night?"

"Of course. Ron and I got a little bored and took a short drive up to Arnold's Knoll. It was so beautiful up there. We could see all the way across the valley to the West Hills. And the stars, Daddy, you would have loved the stars. Pinpoint clear, like diamonds scattered across black velvet."

Maude placed a stack of freshly made pancakes in front of him. "Here are your flapjacks, Mr. Bob. Your eggs will be ready in a jiffy—fried and over easy, right?"

"One of these mornings I'm going to ask for a poached egg, just to confuse you, Maude. Do you even know how to poach an egg?"

The woman grinned. "Mr. Bob, you don't like poached eggs—scrambled maybe, but not poached."

"You know me too well, you surely do. Please don't ever retire! What would I do without you?"

Every now and then, when her sciatica acted up, Maude vowed to retire come Christmas. Yet every year Christmas would come and go, and Maude would still be fixing his breakfast come January. He truly didn't know how he could manage the two-story ranch house without her.

Bob poured boysenberry syrup on his pancakes and added a generous scoop of whipped cream. As he placed the serving spoon back in the bowl of whipped cream, he glanced out of the corner of his eye at Bri and sighed. Somehow she'd turned his intended lecture on being more responsible into a study of the night sky, a love they shared. As a tiny girl, he would heft her onto his shoulders and hike to the top of the ridge behind their property to watch the phases of the moon and the seasonal changes in the stars. Before she could count to ten, the girl could spot the Big Dipper and count the stars in Orion's sword.

He shook his head to remove the rosy-tinted memories. Nineteen years old or not, a call was a matter of courtesy and respect! Sooner or later, he would need to remind her again to call home when she would be staying out late, but not this morning. He hated to ruin the tender mood between them.

As if reading his mind, Bri quipped, "Daddy, I'm sorry. I was so busy getting ready for the show, I forgot to charge my cell phone."

"And Ron's?"

"He left his phone at home in the pocket of his work shirt. In fact, his mom almost put it through the wash!" She placed her hand on his forearm. "Don't worry, Daddy. We were a good little boy and girl last night. Nothing happened, I promise. You do trust me, don't you?"

"You, I trust; your teenage hormones, I do not trust," he growled.

She laughed at his all-too-familiar spiel. "Oh, Daddy, you are so old-fashioned. I love you for it. But you don't need to worry about Ron. He respects you too much to do anything that might disappoint you, even if sometimes I'd like him too."

Bob choked on his pancake. "Brianna Marie Austin!"

"Oh, Daddy, I'm teasing!" She glanced toward Maude. "Are those eggs ready? I am starving this morning!"

"Almost, Honey Bee," the housekeeper chortled. "Almost."

A pickup truck roared to a stop outside the kitchen. The door swung open. Elizabeth burst into the room, dropping a grocery bag of vegetables on the counter by the sink. "Here's a few summer squash and cukes from my garden, Miss Maude. Have you ever tried squash enchiladas? I made some for Kenny last night. They were pretty good, if I must say so myself. Oh, yes, I brought enough for you to take some home to fix for your hubby as well."

Bob rose to his feet and kissed her on the cheek. "Good morning, Bette. Thanks for the veggies. Come join us for breakfast. Tell Ken to come on in. I'm sure we have more than enough for both of you, don't we, Maude? Blueberry pancakes," he coaxed.

"Thanks, but no thanks, Dad. We've already eaten. I'm here to go over the plans for the east forty with you. Those trees are still not thriving as they should. I think we need to plow them under and plant new ones, maybe mandarins or Cuties. Cuties are popular this year."

"Where is Ken?"

"He and the team are trimming the suckers and cutting back dead wood down along the river. They've been at it since sunup. With this heat wave, he wants to knock off work before the height of the heat hits." She leaned on the back of the empty chair across from her father. "Oh, Bri. Great job last night; best yet, in fact."

"Thanks, Bette." Bri cleaned her plate and reached for the serving of eggs Maude had brought to the table. "I didn't know you were there."

"Ken and I didn't stay after the play ended. He knew he'd have to get up before the sun this morning. So Dad, I'll wait for you in the office."

"OK, hon. I'll be there in a moment."

Bette strode from the kitchen as he wolfed down his fried eggs.

"Daddy, may I talk with you later as well?" Bri asked. "I have something important to tell you."

He dabbed his lips with his table napkin and rose to his feet. "Sure, honey. Give me an hour or so to take care of the morning's business with your sister and then I'll be free the rest of the morning."

"OK, Daddy." She blew him a kiss as he left the room. As he disappeared from view, a pout formed on her lips. *Of course, first things first—important business with Bette, and then a few minutes for me.*

CHAPTER FOUR

Moment of Decision

The aroma from melted butter and frying eggs in the heavy iron skillet lingered in the kitchen air as Maude turned to face Bri.

"OK!" Maude posed like a Marine sergeant, with her hands on her ample hips, a spatula in one hand, and a dishtowel in the other. Her snowy white hair drawn into a tight wad at the nape of her neck, she arched one of her bushy white eyebrows and glared. "What's up with you this morning?"

Bri blinked and flashed the housekeeper the most innocent smile she could contrive. "Why, whatever do you mean?"

"You know what I mean. You might fool your papa with your unusually cheerful morning demeanor, but I've known you for too many years. You are never chipper at this hour. Something besides pancakes and eggs is cookin' on your burners."

The girl feigned surprise. "Can't a girl be happy the morning after a successful performance?"

Maude narrowed her gaze. "You were good last night, I'll give you that. But something else is happening in that fertile brain of yours. You can't fool me, young lady. By the way, I saw you sneak into the house as I pulled into the driveway this morning. Five o'clock? Out at such an hour? What were you thinking?"

Bri put her finger to her lips. "Oh, *sh-sh-sh.* Please don't tell Daddy. He'd fallen asleep at his desk. I didn't have the heart to awaken him."

The housekeeper, who'd been like a mother to the girl following Angie's death, folded her arms and glared. "You and that young man of yours didn't do anything you'll live to regret, did you?"

Bri clicked her tongue and rose to her feet. "Of course not, Miss Maudie, dear. Trust me."

"Oh, I trust you. Sooner or later, I trust you to break your father's heart."

A pout formed on the younger woman's lips. "Miss Maudie, how can you say such a thing?" She paused for an instant and then brightened. "Actually, I am up to something. I'm going to do something that will make him mighty proud of me. You will be too. You wait; you'll see." Popping up from the table, she dabbed her lips with her napkin. Maude's frown deepened as Bri planted a kiss on her cheek. "Gotta go. Got a busy day ahead."

"*Hmmph!* I don't like the sound of that. Keep your nose clean, you little stinker," the housekeeper called as the girl disappeared up the stairs. "Mark my words, you're gonna be the death of your daddy yet."

"If you only knew," the girl mumbled under her breath as she bounded into her bedroom and closed the door. After flipping on the radio to her favorite country FM station, she flung open the double doors of her walk-in closet. Thanks to Maude's organization and maintenance, the folded clothing on the shelves and those hanging on padded hangers could have graced the shelves of any trendy boutique along Rodeo Drive. While Bri would never outwardly brag about her extensive wardrobe, she secretly loved hearing her friends' *ooh*s and *aah*s, especially over the multiple rows of shoes that lined the far wall: spiked heels, ballerinas, glitter sneakers, flip-flops, comfy sandals, shiny pumps, and every length of boot from ankle-high to thigh-high. It was any young woman's wildest fantasy. Yet, in all fairness, she willingly shared her largess with her nearest and dearest of friends.

Bri held a midnight-blue satin evening gown up to her body and examined her reflection in the full-length mirror on the back of the door. The sequins splashed across the bodice of the dress sparkled in the closet's incandescent light. *You, Brianna Marie Austin, are going to take Hollywood by storm!*

As she eyed the rows of dresses and gowns hanging on pink satin, padded hangers, her gaze narrowed. *How will I choose what to take and what to leave behind? My poor little Miata can only carry so many suitcases. Plus, Ron will have a case or two, I suppose. I think I'll just pack the bare essentials I'll need until I find an agent and an apartment. Then once I'm settled, I'll have Daddy mail the rest to me.*

Hauling two matching blue-and-purple paisley print Gucci suitcases from the shelf above the closet door, she tossed them onto her bed. Her hands shook with excitement as she attempted to unzip the larger of the two. *Stop it, Brianna Austin! You know you are making the right choice, regardless of what anyone else thinks. Certainly, Clyde What's-his-name knows more about what it takes to make it in film or TV than anyone here in this Podunk town, even Daddy. His specialty is growing oranges, not building a career in Hollywood! Girl, you can feel stardom in your bones!*

She glanced at the clock on the night stand beside her white French provincial princess-style, canopy bed—8:17 A.M. She giggled at the memory of the Christmas Maude gave her the porcelain clock, its face framed with delicate, pink rosebuds. The note that came with it said, "My name is Sophia, goddess of wisdom. My loud alarm (and no snooze button) should awaken you in time for school each morning. May you always be as wise and as lovely as you are today. Love, Maudie."

Well, awakening me each morning for school will no longer be part of your job description, Miss Maudie, dear. Bri bit her lower lip knowing that directing her sarcasm at the family housekeeper and longtime confidant was unfair. The woman had opened her arms and her heart to a lonely, weepy preteen and had encouraged her after the loss of her mother as she made the frightening transition from childhood to womanhood. Maude had helped her pin her golden locks high on her head as she dressed for her first date, had thrown a lollapalooza high school graduation party, and had celebrated Bri's opening performance in *Beauty and the Beast* by making the girl's favorite carrot cake—enough for the entire cast and crew.

The girl's expression softened as she leaned against the canopy pole at the head of her queen-sized bed. *But to be free, totally free—no one telling me what to do and when to do it—ah . . .* Sighing in anticipation, she amped up the volume of her favorite new singer, Bobbie Jo Brenner, a shoo-in for best new artist of the year at the annual Country Music

Awards in Nashville. Bri closed her eyes for a moment and imagined the testy singer with her incredible mop of red hair, accepting her award. *"I want to thank my parents, my agent, my high school vocal teacher who said I'd never make it . . ."*

Shifting the venue to Hollywood's Oscar night, she imagined giving her own acceptance speech for her first performance in a supporting role at the Oscars. *No, make that a leading role. "I want to thank my director, my producer, and the entire cast and crew. I also want to thank my father and my friend Miss Maude, for believing in me. And of course, Ronnie, who's been with me all the way."* Bette's name crossed her mind. *"And a special thanks to my sister who said I'd never make it as an actress. You did more to inspire me than all my acting coaches, agents, and publicists along the way. See, I told you so!"*

With fresh determination, she rescued a lavender printed hatbox from beneath her bed. Clearing a spot on the bed, she removed the top. One item after another, she examined her stash of acquired treasures—a program autographed by each of the cast and crew from *Beauty and the Beast;* her high school diploma; a pressed rose from her bouquet at her sister's wedding; a program from the piano recital where she botched "Kitten on the Keys"; photos from her eighteenth birthday party; flowers, love notes, and candy wrappers from Ronnie. Upon spotting her baptismal certificate, she paused and remembered how special she had felt that day. She pawed through the various birthday cards and letters of congratulations from her friends until she uncovered the envelope protecting the title to "Mimi," her precious Miata. She traced her forefinger over the bold lettering on the note inside the small gift card. "Dearest Honey Bee, congratulations on a job well done. Enjoy your little 'bug' and drive carefully. This baby has power! Wherever you go, whatever you do, remember I will always love you. Hugs 'n' kisses, Daddy."

Tears sprang up in her eyes as she touched the note to her lips. "Oh, Daddy, I'm so sorry. I know how much I am about to hurt you. Please forgive me. Try to understand. I've got to follow my dream. Someday, I'll make you proud. You wait; you'll see." Returning the note and the ownership title into the small manila envelope, she skipped across the room to her provincial-style lady's desk, opened the drawer, and removed her bankbook. The current tally of her account brought a satisfied grin to her face. *That should feed the wolves at our door for a month or two,* she reasoned.

For a brief moment, she brushed the white Priscilla window curtain aside and gazed down at the swing set in the play yard behind the house. At five, the thrill of swinging high enough to see over the tall, wooden fence into the nearest orange grove thrilled her. At nineteen, the wooden fence represented a mile-high barrier to the big, exciting world beckoning her.

After placing both the car title certificate and her bankbook in one of the side pockets of her smaller suitcase, she shoved the hatbox back under the bed. "There! Now to decide what to take, what to leave, and what to have Daddy ship later!"

A knock sounded on her bedroom door. She straightened. The door swung open without a pause. Maude strode in, her arms full of Bri's share of the week's laundry.

"Here you go, baby girl." Maude's gaze landed on the bed. "Where do you want these put?" She didn't wait for a reply but gestured toward the open luggage. "Just where do you think you're going, Missy? To Sacramento with your papa?"

A snippy retort popped into Bri's mind, but she managed to bite her tongue. When the girl failed to immediately answer, Maude turned down the radio. "Uh-hum! You got stars in your eyes. I saw that so-called Hollywood agent talking with you last night. I was tempted to tell him where he could go, but then I realized you are too smart a girl to fall for an old line like his. Was I right?"

When Bri failed to answer, she snorted, "You're kidding. Does your daddy know?" She clicked her tongue. "Do you know how many blue-eyed blondes with pretty little pouts and curvaceous bodies flit into Hollywood each year expecting to be the next Marilyn Monroe or Greta Garbo?"

"Oh, Maudie, I don't expect it to be easy, but out of a thousand girls, one will make it. Why can't that one be me?"

"Possibly, but what that one girl must sacrifice to become a superstar, is it worth it? Just the other night I heard on TV that within thirty minutes of the time a star-struck girl climbs off the bus in Hollywood, she is picked up by a pimp promising her the moon but enslaving her for life!"

"Oh, Maudie, you and your talk shows! I'm hardly a star-struck teenybopper stepping off a Greyhound bus from Okie-ville, Oklahoma, with a ten-dollar bill in one hand and a cardboard suitcase in the other. Besides, Ronnie is going with me."

The woman scowled. "What a doofus! I thought that boy had more sense than that!"

At the woman's criticism, fire darted from Bri's eyes. "Ronnie loves me. He wants to help me realize my dream! And if you love me and if my daddy truly loves me as much as he says he does, you'll both want the same for me!"

"From where I sit, love has little to do with it, baby girl." Maude gave a snort. "So what did your daddy say when you told him?"

"I haven't exactly told him yet, but I will. Please don't say anything. Let me tell him."

The woman shook her head, "Oh, baby, you can be sure I won't say a word. This is your show. Doubt it all you want, but I do love you, little girl, as much as if you were my own, but if you're thinking of leaving while your daddy is gone to Sacramento without so much as a goodbye, I will say something. I'll not stand by and watch you merely disappear into the night."

Bri straightened to her full five-foot-three height. "I would never do that to him. Besides, I need to get him to release my trust fund."

"Well, praise be for blessings great and small!" Mumbling under her breath, the woman whirled about and stormed from the room, the door slamming behind her.

CHAPTER FIVE

The Confrontation

Her sandy-blond hair tied back in a ponytail, the blue-jean-clad Bette, dressed in her customary, freshly pressed, red-and-white plaid western-style shirt, neatly tucked in at the waist, shoved a sheaf of papers toward her father before dropping into the chair opposite him. "I'm handing this directly to you so it won't get lost in your overflow box like last time. It's the bill for the tree trimming last week. Jerry needs to be paid as soon as possible. His wife, Lilly, is back in the hospital for another round of chemo, you know. Even with the health coverage 3 B's Orchards provides, the co-pay can break any budget." She gazed about the cluttered desktop. "Daddy, you really need to hire a secretary to organize your life. I can't believe this mess. How do you ever find anything?"

"Probably so, but believe it or not, I have a system. Maybe when I get back from Sacramento, I'll find a secretary who won't bug me to death. As for Jerry, you're right. When your mama was ill, I thought we'd go under for sure. But somehow, with the help of neighbors and the good Lord, the 3 B's Orchards made it. It took ten years to get back on our feet again, but we did it, thanks in no small part to your careful bookkeeping over the last few years, by the way."

Her face softened with satisfaction. "I just did what I could."

"And it was and still is appreciated. Pray for me that I can horse trade the state government into releasing more water to help get the valley citrus growers through the next few months—"

"Along with the walnut and pistachio growers, the cotton and strawberry farmers, the list goes on. I don't know what those lawmakers in Sacramento are thinking. This valley feeds one half of the population of this country. But we can't do that without water!" She rose to her feet, rounded the desk, and placed a kiss on his balding forehead. "I'd better be going. Oh, Daddy, if anyone can horse trade for the release of more water for the valley, you can. You could charm the rattle off a sidewinder." She laughed. "I'll be back tomorrow morning with a copy of the new contract for the fruit haulers."

"And I'll give you the privilege of announcing the promised raise to the field hands."

"*Tsk!* You do realize the other citrus growers in the area will not be happy with your generosity, don't you?"

Bob chuckled. "You're probably right. Gotta get old George Hastings and the others off their duffs and into the realities of life in the twenty-first century."

Bette knitted her brow, and shook her head, which set her long blond ponytail swinging. "You better watch out, Dad. They'll replace you as head of the Citrus Growers' Association when your contract is up in January."

"Maybe so, but fair is fair. Worse things could happen. Besides, our fruit pickers need to feed and clothe their babies."

"*Tsk!* You are incorrigible. Have you heard any rumors from Sac about what changes are planned for the water allotment this year?"

"Not a word. I'm planning to drive up there tomorrow and wind up a few assembly members' tails." He clicked his tongue. "Politics! I hate politics."

She cast him a sardonic grin. "So I take it that means you are refusing the offer to run for state assemblyman next year?"

"Bet your booties, I am. I don't need the headaches. Now go on, Busy Bee! Get out of here! I have stacks of papers to sign and mail before Henry comes by at two."

As Bob watched his ever-efficient daughter disappear from the room, he paused to listen to the click of her practical leather boots on the red tile floor until the screen door squeaked open and then slammed shut.

A sad smile creased his weathered face. *That child needs to lighten up,* he mused. He knew Bette wasn't happy with his decision to raise the hourly wage of his workers. Instead of saying it to his ever-efficient daughter, he thought to himself, *Sometimes life is about more than the bottom line, but you'll learn that in time, my girl.*

Bette's choice of a husband was as calculated as her major in college and as designed as the neat, precise fit of her blue jeans and the hand-tooled squash blossom imprint on her boots. Bob loved his son-in-law, but he'd never detected the spark between Ken and Bette that he and Angie had enjoyed. At times, alone in the night, he worried that he'd depended on her too much after Angie died. *Did I rob her of her childhood?* he wondered.

When the distinctive, heavy, and jarring beat of music invaded his sanctuary, he glanced up at the ceiling and smiled. Often during the last nine years, he'd wondered if the massive oak beams supporting his turn-of-the-last-century home could survive Bri's growing up years. This morning he chuckled aloud, shook his head, and returned to his computer screen to check his incoming e-mails.

Abruptly, the music stopped. For a moment, all was silent. Bri's bedroom door opened, followed by the rhythmic splat of her flip-flops coming down the oak stair steps. One, two, three, four—the fifth stair squeaked as it had done for the last thirty years—six, seven, eight, nine, ten, followed by a long pause. "Daddy? Are you busy? Can you see me now?"

The door opened a crack. A long, blond curl appeared and then one blue eye, followed by his adorable daughter garbed in a pink and red flowered sundress. She could always bring a smile to his face. Nervously, she adjusted the spaghetti strap of her sundress.

"Of course not. I am never too busy for my Honey Bee." He waved her in.

The young woman crossed the heavy oak floor and placed a white business card on his desk. "Here!" She drew back her hand as if she'd been stung by a hornet.

Bob picked up the card. His eyes narrowed as he read aloud the words, "Clyde Maxwell, talent scout."

He continued to study the words. "*Hmm . . .* Who is this guy? Where'd you get this?"

"Last night, after the final curtain call, Mr. Maxwell handed it to me. He said I have star quality and if I were ever in town, meaning Hollywood, I should look him up." She paused to inhale deeply. "Daddy, I know you planned for me to go to college in the fall, but I really want to go to L.A. and pursue an acting career."

Her father shook his head and removed his reading glasses from his nose. "Honey Bee, you can't be serious. Agents like your Mr. Maxwell are a dime a dozen. They hand out these cards to star-struck kids around the country like favorite uncles pass out Hershey's Kisses to five-year-olds."

Her lips narrowed into a pout. "Are you saying that Mr. Maxwell was lying, that I'm not good enough to make it in Hollywood?"

"Honey Bee, I think you're fabulous and so do all our friends, but there's a world of difference between the local critics of our little production company and the big time. I thought you were enrolling in the community college. A semester or two would help you to discover what other interests you might have. Classes start next month."

She dropped into the straight-backed wooden chair across from him. "I already know what I truly want to do. On stage, I come alive. Besides, I don't think going to college and getting a degree, even a two-year degree, is for me. Like it or not, I'm not Bette!"

"No, you're not. And that's OK, but Hollywood can be a scary place for a young woman. What would you do until you could establish yourself in the business? How would you manage? You are a little more than a year from being twenty years old. That's much too young to go to Hollywood alone."

She brightened. "I wouldn't be alone. Ronnie is going with me."

"Ronnie?" If Bob had had false teeth, he would have swallowed them in one gulp. "I thought he planned to attend the police academy in Fresno this fall."

"He did, but he changed his mind."

"Did he change his mind, or did you change it for him?"

Her pout returned. "Daddy! I merely reminded him that time is of the essence for an actress to break into movies, while a few years' wait won't matter as much for him to fulfill his dream of becoming a policeman."

"And just how will the two of you live? Will he work at some fast-food joint while you pound the pavement searching for your big break?" He leaned back in his chair and held his folded hands to his mouth.

"Oh, that's easy. Ronnie's been saving for his tuition and I have

Grandpa's trust fund. I figure between the two of us, we'll have enough to live on until I can get started."

"Your grandfather's trust fund? You must be twenty-one before you are eligible to touch that. In two years, you will have finished junior college and will be well on your way to a four-year degree."

She leaped to her feet. "I'm not your precious Bette! And I never will be! The last thing I wish to do is to spend my life putting little numbers in little boxes on a spreadsheet. I can't think of anything more boring!" The full skirt of her sundress swooshed about her knees as she whirled in a circle. "Daddy, I want to dance, to laugh, and to live my life in wild abandon, not sit in some four-by-four-foot office cubicle!"

He returned his gaze to the card in his hand. "Honey Bee, two years. Is that so long?" He paused. "Remember when you were a little girl learning to swim? Remember how instead of letting me teach you a few basic strokes in the shallow end of the pool, you ran to the edge and leaped into the deep end? You almost drowned. As a result, you were afraid to enter the water for at least a year. All I'm asking is that you take the next two years to discover the options that are out there for you before you leap into the deep end of life."

"No!" She stomped one foot and shook her curls in protest. "If I'm ever going to make it as an actress, my time is now. I just feel it." She slammed the palm of her hand onto the edge of his desktop. "Daddy, are you going to help me or not? I know you can override the age restriction on my trust fund if you want to. I'm not asking you for any of *your money*. This money is mine!"

Her emphasis on "your money" cut his heart to the quick. Didn't she know it wasn't about the money? Didn't she realize he would give her everything he owned to protect her from the pain and disappointments in store for her if she took this pathway?

"No, your grandfather's trust fund isn't yours until you turn twenty-one. Knowing my father, he had good reasons for stipulating that age."

"Dad, you know that I know that one trip to your lawyer's office and you could get the age requirement on the trust voided."

Bob bit his tongue, for he knew she was right.

"The only reason you don't want to release the fund is because of the portion of the business willed to me. You and my darling sister might need to take a financial loss."

"Honey, do really believe that?"

She turned her face from the pain she saw in his eyes.

"Bri, you have it all wrong. I don't care about the money; I care about you. I love you so much that I don't want to see anything bad happen to you."

She shook her head and clicked her tongue. "Weak, Dad, weak. As if bad things don't happen to people here in the valley—every day, in fact."

"There's a difference—"

"Yeah, here in the valley you can keep tabs on me. Family, friends, and neighbors report to you almost every breath I take. I hate living in this small town. Don't you understand? I need to be free!"

He reached his hand toward her. "Free to do what? You're right; I don't understand. You come and go as you please. You have everything any girl your age could want, and more."

"That's just it. You still think of me as your little girl. I am a woman now. I need to make my own choices. And becoming a star is my choice. You need to know that with or without my trust fund, I am going to Hollywood—not next year or the year after, but right now—this week, in fact. And you can't stop me. I am legally of age, remember?"

His eyes filled with tears. He wasn't sure which barb hurt the most, her accusing him of keeping her from her dreams or of not wanting to release the trust fund due to the financial damage it could possibly bring to 3 B's Orchards. "Do you know the sacrifices you'll be forced to make? Choices that will go against everything your mother and I taught you? You can't imagine how unscrupulous some of the people in the entertainment industry can be. It pains me to think you may lose some of the beauty of who you really are."

Slowly, as if he'd aged ten years during their short exchange, he rose to his feet. Leaning on the edge of his desk, he sighed. "This seems like such a hasty decision on your part. Perhaps we should take a little time to think about this, pray about it before doing anything rash."

"You think about it; you pray about it. I've done all the thinking and praying I intend to do. My bags are packed. I'm scheduled to pick Ronnie up tomorrow morning at seven."

"How does Ron's mother feel about this?"

Bri lifted her chin defiantly. "Ronnie loves me. He's a man, not a momma's boy; he makes up his own mind. Now, will you release my trust fund or not?"

The clock gonged twelve times. The aroma of Maude's salsa bubbling on the kitchen stove wafted down the hall and into the room. "What's the rush? Why don't you invite Ron for lunch, or maybe for dinner tonight, so we can discuss this further?"

"There's nothing to discuss, Daddy. I am not going to miss my golden shot at stardom." She snatched the business card off the desktop. "I'm going with or without your blessing. For that matter, I am going even if you talk Ron out of going with me. I am going!" Her blue eyes flashed with volatile passion.

"Yes, I suppose you will." His shoulders slumped forward; he ran his fingers through his graying hair. "Fine. Though it's against my better judgment, I will make an appointment for this afternoon with Mr. Toomey, our attorney, but only if you promise to sit down with him and listen to his advice."

"Sure, whatever, but he won't change my mind, I promise you that."

To her father, the space between them could be a one hundred-foot deep chasm. He stood and reached for her hands. At first, she resisted, but then she allowed him to draw her close. "Oh baby, please know I will be praying every hour of every day that God will send a bevy of angels to protect you and give you an extra measure of wisdom."

Seeing the tears rolling down his cheeks, she set her jaw and wiped one from her own eye.

"Go with God, my precious one. Go with God."

CHAPTER SIX

The Grapevine

Stuffed to its roof, if such a space exists in a tiny sports car, the Miata leaped out of the driveway. Bri gritted her teeth and jammed her foot down on the gas pedal, sending shards of gravel in her wake. The sight in her rearview mirror of her father being supported by her sister, Ken, and Maude—all with tearstained faces—failed to weaken Bri's resolve.

Tears streamed down Ron's mother's cheeks as the widow waved goodbye from her front porch. Ron stared straight ahead, displaying no emotion as his mother's Mediterranean-style cottage disappeared from view. The Miata had barely turned south on 99 when rain clouds moved in from the northwest, enveloping the young couple in a world of painfully abject silence. Seeing misery in Ron's eyes brought a scowl to her face. The girl knitted her brow more tightly. She hated feeling guilty for being the cause of Mrs. Chaney's tears. In truth, Bri hated ever feeling guilty about anything. She almost found it impossible to admit to any mistake, whether buying the wrong pair of shoes or snarling at a friend.

Upping the volume on the radio to blot out her disturbing thoughts, Bri comforted herself with the dream of how proud Mrs. Chaney would be when she and Ron flew her to Hollywood for Bri's first Academy Award ceremony.

She whipped the car off the highway at the last gas station before the interstate began its climb over the Tehachapi mountain range to the Southern California basin. Stopping beside the first fuel pump available, Bri killed the engine. "I'm hungry and I need a potty break. How about you?"

Robotlike, Ron nodded and climbed out of the car.

"I'm pretty tired. Would you like to drive for a while?" she asked, her voice syrupy sweet, while inside her irritation continued to build against Ron. He hadn't spoken one complete sentence during the two hours since they had left home.

"Sure," he called over his shoulder, and headed toward the restrooms.

"I'll fill the tank while you're gone." She watched him disappear inside the building without a reply. The first droplets of rain fell as she slid her bankcard into the slot on the fuel tank and removed the gas cap from her car.

She finished filling the tank, retrieved her receipt, and entered the small grocery store. In the background, a radio DJ at a local station promoted a junior rodeo to "all you folks in radio-land." The phony Texas-style dialect brought a smile to her face as she placed a large bag of tortilla chips and a jar of salsa on the counter. *Made in New York City,* she mused as she read the label.

"I need to use the little girls' room," she said to the distracted clerk, who was busy texting a friend. "When the guy I'm traveling with comes out of the men's room, place his purchases on my tab." She whirled about and hurried toward the ladies' room. As she reached the door, Ron emerged from the men's facility. She pasted on a bright smile. "Get whatever you're hungry for—my treat."

He passed her without making eye contact and snarled, "I can purchase my own snacks."

"Well . . . OK. Whatever . . ."

"Yeah! Whatever!"

Irked, she shook her head as he strode to the drink machine and filled a giant cardboard cup with ice and soda. Sooner or later, they'd need to talk about his feelings. For her, later was better than sooner. The fact that the rain had quickly intensified from a drizzle to a deluge didn't help her mood either. Her dream for this day hadn't included a rainstorm or Ron's bad mood. She'd envisioned her Hollywood entrance including cruising down Rodeo Drive with the sun shining and the top down on her beloved Mimi, a bright-print silk scarf around her neck and her long blond curls blowing in the afternoon breeze. That's how it was supposed to be.

When she returned, Ron had slipped behind the wheel, set his giant cup of soda in the drink holder, and revved up the engine. As she opened the car door, he ended a conversation with an unknown caller and dropped his cell phone in the pocket of his shirt.

"Who was that?" she asked as she climbed into the car and closed the door.

"I was talking to my mother, if that's all right with you," he snarled.

Bri buckled her seat belt and folded her arms tightly about her waist.

The rhythmic swish of the windshield wipers filled the silence between them. Ron cranked on the air-conditioner to clear the fog from the windows. With semitrucks and large SUVs speeding past the low-riding sports car, the road became more and more difficult to see, forcing them to slow to a crawl over the Grapevine. Whenever a giant semi passed, the tiny motor vehicle swerved as if swamped in an outrageous, free-for-all car wash.

A motorcyclist, his yellow slicker flapping in the wind, zipped past them on the right. "Watch out!" she gasped.

"I saw him! Do you want to drive?"

"No." She wilted further down into the passenger seat as if wishing to be invisible. She was bewildered, as she'd never before heard such a snarky tone from Ron. On the contrary, he was consistently the happiest person she knew.

Bri wondered about the conversation he'd had with his mom, but was afraid to ask. At the moment, his silence seemed preferable to his biting sarcasm.

She recalled the disappointed and fretful expression on her father's face as she kissed him goodbye, unlike the stoic, disapproving look on her sister's face. Not so long ago, the two girls were inseparable. Bette had mothered her, *or better yet, smothered me,* Bri thought. The three had joined hands and had prayer as they had done every time they would be separated from one another. Her father's pleas for God to watch over his Honey Bee were tinged with pain. Reluctantly, her father had released her hand and searched her face as if hoping to find a note of reluctance to leave.

"You know you can come home any time, don't you?" her father whispered in her ear. Tears glistened in his eyes as he crushed her into his arms. "Anytime. And should you need anything, just call me. Don't let silly pride get in the way of common sense."

Pride? Pride! I'm not proud, merely determined. Seeing her father's tears, she almost weakened; almost chickened out. But a surge of rebellion bubbled up in her heart. She'd come too far to quit now without losing face. She steeled her resolve against his display of emotions. Hadn't she spent their last evening together determined to make him see that she could go it on her own, that she could make it in the circus arena of Hollywood? She would become a star. She would be the exception to the rule of the theater jungle that wrecked other hapless girls' dreams.

When he'd suggested she spend a few additional days praying in order to know God's will for her, she'd steeled her heart. Her plans didn't include waiting on the will of her father's unseen and unseeing Deity, the One who'd been deaf to her pleas as her mother lay dying. She tuned out her father's pleas with visions of swirling sequined skirts, red carpet runways, and paparazzi flash. While some stars came to resent the media's intrusion, she wouldn't. She would bask in the glow of all the attention she would soon earn.

The silence between her and Ron continued during the hours it took to drive over the mountains. At the south end of Santa Clarita, she suggested they stop at a fast-food place. "There's not much in the way of fast food between here and L.A.," she reminded Ron.

Without a word, he pulled off the interstate and drove into the nearest restaurant parking lot. "Do you want to eat in or do take-out?" he asked.

"I'd kind of like to eat here, if you don't mind." Bri swallowed hard. *This is so unlike him. Perhaps he will begin to talk over a burrito and drink,* she reasoned.

He placed their order while she settled into an empty booth. She stared out of the plate-glass window into a swirl of puddles, muddy vehicles, and falling rain. Her eyes misted as she blocked out the irritating voice of a DJ on a local country-western radio station promoting an upcoming demolition derby.

Ron set the tray on the table, removed the food from the tray, and slid into the bench across from her. "I hope you like what I got you. They're frying up a fresh batch of tortilla bowls. So I got you a couple of bean tacos instead."

"Fine," she mumbled as she unwrapped the first taco he'd placed in front of her.

"I can go back and get you the tortilla bowl if you like."

"No, no, this is fine, Ron, honest. This is fine." She lifted her gaze to meet his. "What isn't fine is the two of us. Talk to me. Tell me what is happening. I can't bear your silence."

A crooked smile coursed his lips. "You really don't know, do you?"

"No, I don't."

"It's all my fault anyway. I should have stood up to your harebrained idea from the start, and I didn't. I never dreamed I'd go this far to please you, Bri."

"But I thought—"

"Thought? That's the problem, you didn't think of what I might want at all. I don't know where I fit in your grand plan. I feel like I'm your sidekick, like Wild Bill Hickok to your Calamity Jane or Robin to your Batman; your bodyguard; your straight man; an accessory to be worn like a Tiffany necklace or a Dior wrap."

She placed her hands on his. "Oh, Honey Bunny, you mean so much to me. Without you to share my successes with, I don't know what I'd do. You complete me."

"I'm not so sure." He turned his face from hers. "Seeing my mom, who is usually as strong as a rock, crumble into uncontrollable tears—I felt so helpless."

"Your mom will be fine. As you say, she's a strong woman, Ron. It's not like she lives as far away as Wisconsin or Kansas. You'll be less than four hours away from her. You can drive up to see her any time, right? This is our time. She wouldn't want to hold you back from reaching your dreams."

"My dreams?" He studied her face for several seconds before he spoke. "Your dreams, you mean."

She tipped her head to one side and raised her left eyebrow. "Look, if you want to change your mind and go back home like a whipped puppy, go ahead. I'll drop you off at LAX and you can catch the next commuter plane north." She clicked her tongue. "But you need to know that alone or with you, I'm going to Hollywood today! What will it be?"

He heaved a deep sigh. "OK. I promised your dad that I would watch over you, so I'll stay for now."

"You promised my dad?" She frowned. "Hey, as you said so eloquently, you are not my bodyguard." She took a bite from her taco. "You are my best friend. If the time comes when you wish to leave, I will release you from the promise you made to my father."

"That's not the issue. I feel honored that he trusts me enough to ask. We vowed to wait 'til marriage to make love. It will be difficult to maintain that vow while living together day after day. But as much as I love you, I'm certainly not ready to get married, are you?"

She blinked in surprise. "Marriage? No, of course not. I've got to get my career off the ground before we do that. Maybe a year from now, but marriage would be a giant mistake right now."

"I agree." He shook his head and bit his lower lip.

"What? What?"

"You are such a child. You really don't know how difficult it will be to live together in a one-room flat and maintain a non-intimate relationship, do you? I'm only human." He paused and reddened. "Sometimes, Bri, you can be so naive. I am sincerely afraid for you."

She clicked her tongue. "I am not naive, Ron. I'm not a child. I do understand how life works."

He lifted his gaze toward the ceiling. "Trust me on this. You are such a child." He stuffed the last bite of taco into his mouth. "We'd better hit the road. The rain is coming down harder, and we need to find a place to stay tonight."

Piqued by his demeaning analysis of her, she shoved the last of her second taco into her mouth, chewed it, and dotted her lips with the paper napkin. "Fine. But as for tonight's accommodations, I booked a room for us at the Hollywood Western if that meets your fancy or, should I say, if you can control your prurient desires." She handed him the street address for the hotel. "And yes, it has two beds!" she snapped. Grabbing her purse, she leaped to her feet, whirled about, and strode toward the ladies' room. "Like it or not, I am making a pit stop before we hit the road, as you put it."

She emerged from the restroom to find Ron waiting in the car with the engine running. Opening the door with as much force as she dared, she climbed into the passenger seat. *If he wants quiet, I'll give him quiet!*

The car door slammed with a thud.

She curled up as best she could in the bucket seat, turned to face the side window, and closed her eyes. *The whole world has conspired to dampen the Disneyesque image of my arrival in Los Angeles: the rain, Maude's unwelcomed advice, Daddy's warnings, Bette's silent censure, Ron's mother's tears, Ron himself, and oh, yes, don't forget the rain! Is this a portent of things to come from You, Lord?*

CHAPTER SEVEN

Home Alone

The clock gonged five. It had been a very long afternoon for Bob. The silence of the house had closed in on him ever since Bri had left. He'd lost count of how many times he had glanced toward the clock's copper hands as they wound their way around the clock's walnut face. A few minutes after five thirty, Maude announced that she was leaving for the day. "Have you heard from Bri yet? They should be there by now."

He shook his head.

"The hubby and I are going to the farmers' market tonight. Anything you'd like us to pick up for you?"

"Not that I can think of. Thanks. Have fun." A memory of Angie wearing her wide-brimmed straw hat and her yellow-and-white sunflower sundress, with her zebra-striped shopping bag over her wrist popped into his mind. Their Tuesday night outings had always included the local farmers' market. When he closed his eyes, he could almost see their two daughters bouncing ahead of them like fawns from stall to stall sampling the giveaways being offered. He started at the sound of Maude's voice. He'd forgotten she was still present.

"I made a potato salad and a bowl of your favorite black beans for your dinner tonight. Microwave the beans for one minute at half power when you're ready to eat. Also, I grated some cheddar cheese and sweet onions to top off the beans, just as you like 'em."

"You spoil me, Maude, dear. Tell that hubby of yours I said he's a lucky man." He glanced up from the papers scattered across his desk, the same papers he'd been reading hours earlier before Bri drove away.

"Are you going to be all right, Mr. Bob?" She inched into the room. "Is Bette coming over to be with you tonight? If she is, I can stay a while longer until she gets here."

"Thank you, but no. I'll be fine. Bette and Ken have other plans tonight, I'm sure." He pursed his lips. "I'm thinking of calling Ron's mom, to see how she's doing."

Maude wrung her hands nervously. "That would be nice, Mr. Bob. I'm sure she'd like that. There's enough food for two," the woman encouraged.

He shot a knowing grin at her. His housekeeper had been incorrigible over the years since Angie's death, trying to get him "married off," as she put it. That poor Mrs. Chaney was a good ten years older than he and had a trace of skin whiskers on her chin didn't deter his longtime housekeeper and friend. He shook his head. "A phone call will suffice, Maudie. A phone call will suffice."

The woman shrugged her shoulders, turned, and left. He waited until he heard her pickup truck exit the driveway before he wandered into the kitchen and opened the refrigerator. He grabbed an open bottle of orange juice from the top shelf, removed the cap, and took a swig. Recalling how both Maude and Bri got after him for drinking from the bottle, a wry smile crossed his lips. He re-closed the bottle and returned it to the shelf.

After fixing his plate of food as directed, he crossed the hall into the family room and sat in his favorite easy chair in front of the fifty-inch television. He set his plate on the side table, grabbed the remote control, and flicked on the television to catch the evening weather report.

"Tonight, the unseasonably warm temperatures have dropped, thanks to the marine air coming in from the Northern California coast. The weather pattern that brought much needed rain to the Central Valley today has moved to the east and south through the Sierra Nevada Mountain passes, leaving behind blue skies and comfortably cooler temperatures for the rest of the week. Earlier today, torrential rains made it slow going over the Grapevine and into the L.A. Basin, drenching the Southern California megalopolis with several inches of unexpected rain."

Worried about how Bri and Ron had fared driving over the mountains, Bob removed his cell phone from his shirt pocket. While the blond weather girl with the toothpaste-white smile and snapping blue eyes reported the forecast for the following week, he said to the phone's automated voice, "Call Bri." The instant before the call went through, he clicked it off. The last thing he wanted was for his daughter to interpret his concern as an attempt to keep tabs on her.

The newscast broke for what seemed to be an endless string of furniture, pharmaceutical, and automobile commercials. Muting one high-pressure salesman hawking retirement insurance, he instructed his phone to call Ron's mother. After several rings, he heard the woman's voice. "Hello?" Her voice sounded as if she'd been crying.

"Hi, Martha, this is Bob. I'm just wondering how you're doing."

She paused for an instant. "About as well as can be expected. Have you heard from the kids? I heard they're having storms in L.A."

"Haven't heard a word. I called hoping you had."

"Ron called earlier, at the base of the Grapevine, but nothing since. He said the roads were sloppy. But I suppose that by now, they're trying to find a place for the night or having dinner somewhere. Sure hope they made it safely over the mountains." He detected a sniffle at the end of her transmission.

"Yeah. According to the evening news reports, they must've encountered heavy rain the entire way. Martha, are you sure you're all right? Should I come over?"

"No, I'm fine, but thanks for offering. I spent the day weeping and sleeping. I'm sure I'll be awake all night watching *Law & Order* reruns." She gave a chuckle. "How about you? How are you holding up? Are Bette and Ken there with you tonight?"

"No, they have their own lives to live. I'm just vegetating in front of the TV and thought I'd give you a call before *Jeopardy* begins. I know you're a fan. Hey, listen, if you need anything, at any time, day or night, just call me, ya hear?"

"Thanks, but I'm sure I'll be fine. As the old song goes, 'The sun will come out tomorrow.' I appreciate your offer though. And if you hear anything from them, you'll call me?"

At the mention of the song from the musical *Annie,* Bri's first lead role in the local theater, Bob furrowed his brow. "And you do the same, OK?"

"Absolutely." Her voice broke.

"Are you sure you're OK?" he insisted. "Should I drive over to your place?"

"No, no, I'm fine."

"Oh, Martha, I feel so responsible. If I hadn't agreed to break her trust fund . . . If I'd insisted she—"

"It's not your fault. Brianna and Ron are adults, old enough to make their own choices and their own mistakes. All we can do is pray for them—both."

"You are being more gracious than I feel," he admitted. "I should have seen this coming. Bri has always been so pig-headed. Even her mother had to rein in the girl's determination."

"Bob, it is what it is. I better go. I have eggs boiling in a pan on the stove and I don't want to miss the *Jeopardy* theme song. Take care."

"You too, Martha." He clicked the phone off, set it on the stand beside his chair, and sighed. The food on the plate barely looked edible anymore. He took a forkful of beans—cold. The potato salad looked even less enticing. As the theme song for the quiz show began, he shuffled to the kitchen and dumped the food down the garbage disposal. "This house is too quiet!" he announced to the four walls.

Grabbing his truck keys from the hook beside the kitchen door, he bounded out of the house to do what he always did when he needed space to think. It's what he did after the death of his beloved Angie. He'd drive the miles of orchard trails, muddy as they'd be after the day's hard downpour. He'd find comfort being surrounded by his beloved fruit trees. As he turned the key in the ignition, the massive engine roared to life. That's when he realized he could drive every mile of road through his orange groves; he could drive every gravel road between the valley and the Pacific Ocean and back, and not find the peace his spirit craved. He pulled over to the side of one of the roads and laid his head on the wheel. "Bring her safely home, dear Father."

CHAPTER EIGHT

Making the Rounds

Bri rose before dawn, too excited to sleep. She stood in front of the large mirror in the motel room's bathroom. She wanted to allow plenty of time to apply her makeup. No slapping it on and going out the door this morning. Her hand shook as she applied her eyeliner. She studied the familiar face in the mirror. *Should I wear false lashes or opt for a heavy coat of mascara? Should I wear an ingénue pink lipstick to go with my pink and lavender sundress, or a naughty red to offset my form-fitting black leggings and zebra print blouse?* She knew that whatever look she chose had to be perfect. *One never gets to remake a first impression,* she reminded herself.

She glanced over her shoulder at the bevy of flashy outfits that lay strewn about the room. That she could stuff so much clothing into one little Miata amazed even her. Remembering Ron's small duffle bag that he'd stuffed behind the passenger seat brought her a moment of guilt, but only a moment. *This is my adventure. I'm the one who needs a flashy wardrobe.*

She'd just painted her toes and fingernails a passion pink when Ron returned from the hotel's breakfast bar with a bagel and cream cheese, a small plastic bottle of orange juice, and a plate of cold scrambled eggs.

"I hope you like what I brought you." He cleared a space on the coffee table in front of the sofa bed, and then removed two apples, two bananas, and a second bagel wrapped in a paper napkin. "I considered grabbing a few boxes of cereal, too, but we have no way to keep milk cold here in the room."

Bri's stomach growled from hunger, but she eyed the leggings on the foot of the bed. "Thanks, Ron, but if I want to wear those," she pointed to the leggings, "I must have a flat tummy." Seeing the disappointed look on his face, she added, "But an apple should be OK."

"I also picked up a copy of the Actors' Guild trade paper released today." He handed it to her. "The girl at the front desk says that fledgling actors live and die by the information available in this thing."

"That was really thoughtful of you, but I doubt I'll need it. Remember, I have Clyde Maxwell's card. Or was his name Sylvester Maxwell? Or perhaps Clyde Sylvester?" Her laugh tantalized the air like crystal wind chimes in the breeze. "But who knows? It might come in handy later. I thought after I reintroduced myself to Mr. Maxwell that we could look for a small apartment to rent."

Ron nodded in agreement. "That's a good idea, since we can't afford to stay very long in this motel, as nice as it is. What if I make an appointment to meet with a real estate agent while you check in with Mr. Maxwell?"

"Good idea." She grabbed her clothing and disappeared into the bathroom to change out of her flannel PJs. Seconds later, she emerged wearing the zebra print top and black leggings. She slipped her bare feet into the five-inch red pumps and cavorted about the small space like a solo ballerina. She flung her arms into the air. "This is so exciting. I can barely stop shaking. It's really happening, Ronnie! It's really happening!"

"You look great." Ron smiled approvingly. "If that outfit doesn't get Mr. Sylvester's attention, nothing will. While you eat your apple, we'll drive to Sylvester's office."

After an hour of inching through Los Angeles' notorious early morning traffic, Ron found a parking spot two blocks from the address on the card. Bri clung tightly to Ron's hand, feeling grateful that they were on speaking terms again. The couple hurried past aging stucco buildings; some boarded up; some graffitied with gang symbols; all with wrought iron bars on the first-floor windows. Finally, they found the address on the card.

Bri inched closer to his side. "This can't be right. It's a dump," she hissed. "Are you sure we're in the right place?"

He craned his neck to catch the letters on the street sign at the corner and then at the numbers above the door. "Yeah, that's what's printed on the card."

Two picture-perfect blue-eyed blondes, dressed in spike heels and outfits designed for females two sizes smaller, sashayed up the street. They paused before the door and pressed the call button on the doorjamb.

"Pardon me," Ron began, "is this the office of the Maxwell Talent Agency?"

The taller girl cast him a coy, sideways smile while the shorter of the two sized up Bri. "Yes, it is, good lookin'," the first girl cooed.

"Really?" Bri twisted her mouth in disgust.

"Aw, it's not so bad once you get upstairs." The second blonde opened the door. "You're new in town, aren't you? Let me guess, you're from Kansas or maybe Oklahoma. I'm Desiree. I'm from Cleveland, Ohio, and Mauri here is from Seattle. That's in Washington State, you know."

A condescending smile swept across Bri's face. "I know. Actually, I'm from the Central Valley."

Desiree cast her a quizzical look. "Oh, but what state are you from?"

Ron glanced away, but not before Bri caught the tiny smirk on his face.

Mauri, the other girl, clicked her tongue. "That's California, Desiree, California."

"Oh, is that near Riverside or San B?"

"No, California's Central Valley is a ways north of here," Ron quipped as he held the door for all three girls to enter the darkened hallway. As they climbed the narrow staircase to the second floor office, Desiree maintained a running monologue.

"I was working at a local pizza parlor in Cleveland when I got fired for dropping a giant fresh-from-the-oven pizza upside down in some guy's lap. He was a jerk anyway! The next morning, I told my mom I'd had it and I was leaving for Hollywood." The girl sighed. "That was five months ago. I've done real good, I think. I've dressed as the Statue of Liberty, a chicken for a fast-food joint, and a clown for some snot-nosed kid's party, though my best part yet was playing the elevator operator in the flick *Upside Down*. You've seen it, right?" She didn't wait for Ron or Bri to reply. "It was just a bit part with only one line but hey, ya gotta start somewhere, right? Going up?"

Mauri led the way to the door with the sign "Maxwell Talent Agency" painted on the translucent glass in the door. "You'll like Maxie, that's what all the girls call him."

"All the girls?" Ron asked. "Doesn't he represent any male talent?"

Mauri shrugged her shoulders. "Not really."

Ron eyed Bri and then glanced toward the other girl. "Doesn't that bother you?"

Again, the girl shrugged and led the way into a large waiting room lined with metal folding chairs. In each of the available chairs sat a cookie-cutter version of Mauri and Desiree. Bri felt the calculating eyes of every girl follow her across the room.

"Hi, Mauri, Desiree," called out a middle-aged receptionist with dyed red hair piled atop of her head, who sat behind a black metal desk. "There's nothing on the docket this morning. Who are your new friends?"

Bri straightened her shoulders and lifted her chin to appear as put-together as possible. Her stomach churned as she strode across the tiled floor and cast a broad—and what she hoped to be confident—smile at the woman. She handed her the agent's calling card. "Hi, my name is Brianna Austin. I'd like to make an appointment to speak with Mr. Maxwell, please."

The woman briefly glanced at the card. "Let me guess. You're here to become the next Hollywood femme fatale, right?"

Ron stepped up to Bri's side and slid his arm about her waist. "Mr. Maxwell said we were to look him up if we ever found ourselves in Los Angeles."

"I know the drill. He saw you, honey," she said, looking toward Bri, "in a local production of who knows what—"

"*Beauty and the Beast,*" Bri inserted.

"Of course, *Beauty and the Beast.*" She rolled her eyes toward the ceiling.

Mauri leaned onto the edge of the desktop. "Give the kid a break, Agnes."

The woman gestured to the waiting crowd. "How many of these hopefuls can give you the same spiel?" She sat back down behind the desk. "Everyone arrived in this office with the same stars sparkling in their eyes that dim the longer they stay. Go home, little girl. This business will eat you alive."

"Agnes! Cut it out! Just because you didn't make it big twenty-some years ago, doesn't mean none of us will." The woman glared at Desiree as the younger woman turned toward Bri. "Don't listen to her. Agnes is strung out on booze this morning."

"Yeah," Mauri interrupted. "Just tell our friend what she needs to do before she can get started."

Agnes heaved an impatient sigh. "Do you have your portfolio?"

"Portfolio?" Bri asked.

"Your collection of headshots." The older woman gave an impatient sigh and muttered, "Amateurs." Pasting on an empty smile, she continued, "And obviously, you need an agent—that's why you're here. You can't work without one." She withdrew a packet from the side drawer of her desk and handed it to Bri. "Here! Come back when you've completed all the forms." When she caught Ron's disapproving glare, she cast him a provocative grin. "How about you, big boy? The industry is always looking for hunks like you."

Ron returned her grin. "Sure, why not? I'll take one of those packets." Immediately, she obliged.

"And all these ladies here?" he asked.

"Hoping for a casting call this morning. When Mr. Maxwell comes in, he will send the most promising ones out on cattle calls; that means, 'In for a penny, in for a pound.' "

He rolled his eyes toward Bri. "Guess we'd better fill out the information sheets." He turned back toward the receptionist. "Where do you advise we go for headshots?"

"Well, that depends on how much money you're willing to spend. Obviously, the more you spend, the better the shots will be. You can pay anywhere from two hundred dollars to two thousand and beyond." She placed her elbows on the desktop and pointed. "In your packet, you'll find a list of recommended photographers and their base prices. Come back when you're ready to work."

Outside on the street, Ron and Bri headed for the parked Miata when Mauri called, "Hey, do you guys have a place to stay tonight? We have an empty room where you could bunk until you get settled."

"Really?"

"It's a pretty neat place."

"What do you think?" Bri turned to Ron.

"Sure, why not?" he nodded.

Bri turned toward the girls. "Last night we stayed in a motel near here. That gets expensive fast."

Desiree laughed. "For sure. Do you have wheels? Everyone needs a car in L.A."

"Oh, yeah." Bri pointed up the street. "We parked my car two blocks away."

"I know the place. We'll get our jalopy and meet you there." Mauri gave a wave and turned in the opposite direction. Several horns beeped when the two girls ran across the oncoming traffic to the far side of the street.

"Aggressive drivers," Ron muttered.

Minutes later, Bri paid the parking attendant and tossed her keys to Ron. "Here. I don't want to drive in L.A. traffic quite yet. Perfect day to put the top down, don't you think?"

He obliged. They climbed into their waiting vehicle as their new friends drove up in an aging green, four-door Honda sedan. "Wow! Do you ever have wheels!" Desiree shouted. "Why don't we follow you back to your hotel so you can pick up your luggage, then follow us home?"

Ron signaled an OK. To Bri, he added, "I hope we're doing the right thing. These two could be leading us into a scam of some kind."

Bri chuckled at the thought. "Yeah, you could be right, or they could be exactly what they seem to be, two girls trying to be nice." She let the breeze tousle her golden locks as Ron guided the Miata through the busy traffic to the motel parking lot. While they loaded their luggage into the car, Mauri and Desiree watched.

With the sun at their backs, they followed the Honda due west. Bri gasped at the first view of the Pacific Ocean. The clutter of businesses made way for rows of palm trees and sandy beaches as they neared the famous Malibu area. "Isn't it beautiful? Imagine! We can stroll down by the water every day if we want."

"Yeah. But who knows where their house is and what we'll encounter when we get there."

"Oh, don't be a spoilsport. Consider this part of our adventure."

The Honda turned down a narrow lane lined with modest-looking beach houses. At the end of the lane, as the road angled away from the ocean, the Honda stopped and the two girls hopped out. "We're home!" Desiree shouted. "Park anywhere."

Bri couldn't believe her eyes when she took in the size of the sprawling three-story stucco home. "This is your place?"

"Ah, no. It belongs to Sam Locke's dad. Sam's a great gal. You'll like her."

Ron gazed at the flight of stairs leading to the house's main floor. "Are you sure she's not going to mind our being here?"

"Are you kidding? She's been talking about getting a couple of new roommates. The place has seven bedrooms and eight bathrooms. The best part is . . ." Desiree threw open the carved mahogany double doors revealing a massive kitchen and great room, floor-to-ceiling windows, and a deck facing the ocean. "I could sit out there and stare at the waves for hours."

Behind her, Mauri called, "Hey Sam, are you home? She's probably out on location in Palm Desert for a commercial shoot she's doing."

Captivated by the view, Bri and Ron dropped their luggage on the tile floor and gazed out the giant plate-glass sliding doors, but not before Desiree noted Bri's expensive luggage.

"Love your matching suitcases. You can stay the night until Sam returns. And if she likes you, she'll make arrangements with you regarding rent. But for now, you'll be our guests." Desiree waved toward Ron. "You can put your and Bri's luggage upstairs in the last bedroom on the right. It's been vacant since Anne Briggs returned home to Georgia last month. Sorry it doesn't have an ocean view."

Mauri caught the slight grimace on Ron's face.

"Same room?" he asked.

She brightened at the prospect that he might be an available male. "If you two want more privacy, the connecting room next door is also empty. The two rooms share a bathroom and a hot tub."

Bri strolled through the giant sliding doors onto the deck. The sound of seagulls flying overhead and the waves lapping the sandy shore greeted her. Her eyes misted. "This view is amazing. It's like I can see all the way to Hawaii or even China. When I make it big, this is just the kind of place I want to own. Seven bedrooms? Does anyone else live here with you guys?"

"Sure. Sam and her significant other, Leo Briggs, share the master bedroom. Leo's a masseuse." Desiree leaned against the metal railing of the second-story deck. "Wendy Fisher rooms across the hall from you. She's a struggling costume designer. And Summer Downy lives at the far end of the hall. Summer is like us, an actress trying to break into the business."

"Wow! It's almost like an exclusive frat club." Bri glanced up at the faceless third-floor windows.

"Yeah. And like frat clubs, we do know how to party," Desiree giggled. "This place really rocks on weekends."

CHAPTER NINE

Calling Home

The telephone on the desk beside Bette's stack of invoices jangled. With slight irritation at the interruption, she put the receiver to her ear. "Three B's Orchards. This is Bette Raab speaking. How may I help you?"

"Bette? This is Ron. Is your father there? I need to speak to him." It had been several weeks since she or her father had heard from Ron or Bri.

"Sorry, he's in Sacramento, wining and dining state legislators today, trying to free up more water for the valley growers. He's supposed to be home in a few hours if his flight doesn't get canceled. So how are things for you guys in Tinseltown? Did my sister land her big movie role yet?"

"Not yet," Ron groaned. "But we're hitting the pavement every morning, circulating our headshots and chasing down cattle calls. Trust me! I now know the meaning of the term 'cattle call.' The casting directors truly make you feel like a piece of fresh meat more than a human being. It's a tough business."

"I imagine so."

Feeling he needed to defend his partner, Ron added, "Bri landed a gig dressed as a taco at the grand opening of a Mexican restaurant in Van Nuys. That's where she is today. She's also picking up extra cash attending high-powered business events."

"Like a paid escort?" Bette interjected. Disbelief filled her voice.

"Not exactly, at least not the sex for hire part like you see on TV. It's her job to 'pretty up the place,' as her agent calls it."

"And you, Ron, how are you doing?"

"I landed my first Hollywood job playing a toothbrush for a toothpaste commercial." He laughed. "I guess I was the skinniest guy there. But the reason for my call is that Bri asked me to have your father send her clothes to our address in Malibu."

"Malibu? You're living in Malibu?" The older sister chuckled. "I would have expected that you'd be living in East L.A."

"Afraid not. We're renting rooms at a friend's beach house. We made a deal with our friend, Sam, who's an actress, and her boyfriend Leo, which will work as long as our money lasts. Everything down here is so expensive. Here's the address. Do you have a pen and paper handy?"

"Yes. Go ahead." She scribbled the address down on a Post-it note and stuck the note along the side of the computer screen. "Got it. It will be the first thing he sees when he comes into the office tonight."

"Great. Thanks. Bri sends her greetings. Tell Ken we said Hi as well."

"You got it. Oh, wait. I just heard Dad's pickup truck pull up outside. Hold on."

The screen door slammed. "Dad? It's Ron on the phone." The thud of a travel case hit the Mexican tile floor outside the open office door. Bob burst into the room. His face glowed as he took the receiver from his older daughter.

"Ron? How are you doing, man? Is Bri there?"

"No, she's out on a job today. She asked me to call you and have you send her clothing. I gave Bette our current address."

"Oh." Bob's voice dropped; his shoulders drooped. He picked up the Post-it note and examined it. "Do you guys have a phone number other than your cell phones? I've tried to call several times, but every call has gone to voicemail."

"I know and I am sorry about that. Bri is sensitive about talking with you. She feels she needs her space right now. I try to honor her wishes, though I do call my mom on a regular basis, as you know."

"Yes, but it's not the same."

"I know. But my mom promises to forward any news to you."

"Thank you. Your mother does a fine job keeping me up-to-date. I'd love to see copies of your and Bri's headshots, if you could send them." Bob recognized a whining note in his voice, but he couldn't help wanting more from his little girl. "Hey, I have a few days free next weekend. I'd love to pop in and surprise Bri. It's her birthday, you know."

"Uh . . ." A long pause followed. "That's probably not a good idea, sir. Bri has two gigs this weekend, a cocktail party and a dinner party. Besides, it's just not the right time."

Bob's heart sank. "And when is the right time?"

"Uh, give her the space she needs. She wants to succeed for you, you know. She wants you to be proud of her."

"I'm proud of her already. I've always been proud of her." Again, Bob could hear the pleading in his voice. He cleared his throat. "I'll ask Maude to box Bri's personal items and send them out in tomorrow's mail. You should have them by the end of the week."

"Thanks, sir. She'll be thrilled."

"Remember, I'm praying for you both. If either of you needs anything, anything at all . . ."

"Yes, sir. I do think Bri could use some of your common sense when it comes to budgeting her trust fund." His voice dropped.

"What do you mean? She should have enough money to live on for a long time, even in L.A."

"Sorry, sir. I shouldn't have said anything. Thanks for looking out for my mother. She really appreciates having you check in on her every now and then. I do too."

"Glad to do it, son. And well, be sure to tell Bri that I love her; I miss her and pray for both of you several times a day."

"Yes, sir. Thank you, sir, I will tell her if she ever slows down long enough to listen to me. Well, gotta go now. We'll talk again soon. Bye."

Bob heard a click and the line went dead. He felt hollow inside, like his lifeblood had been drained out of him. With every call from Ron, he experienced feelings similar to those he'd experienced on the day he held Angie in his arms and felt her last breath escape her body. For comfort, he opened his Bible to Psalm 139. He turned to verses 7–10— a promise he claimed for his precious younger daughter. "Where can I go from your Spirit? Where can I flee from your presence? If I go up to the heavens, you are there; if I make my bed in the depths, you are there. If I rise on the wings of the dawn, if I settle on the far side of the sea, even there your hand will guide me."

Silently, he set his Bible aside and closed his eyes. Under his breath, he vowed, "You may run to the far corners of the earth, little one, but there is nothing you can do nor anywhere you can go to escape from my heart, my God, and my prayers for you."

CHAPTER TEN

Tequila Delights

The citrus yellow Miata breezed into the parking space on the lower level of the beach house. The blare of mariachi music filled the area. Almost without killing the engine, Bri, in her white short-shorts and hot pink, spaghetti-strapped tank top hopped out of the vehicle and bounded up the stairs to the living space. "Ronnie! Ronnie! I got the part! I got the part!"

She smiled at the sight of bikini-clad bodies gyrating to the ear-shattering mariachi music out on the deck. The party had already begun. Tonight the tequila would flow. Dashing up the stairs to the second floor, she shouted over the din, "I got the part! I got the part!"

As Ron, dressed in khaki swim trunks and an army green T-shirt, stepped out of his room, she threw herself into his arms. "Pooh Bear! I got the part. Can you believe it? I got the part!"

He laughed and allowed himself to be whirled around in a circle. "What part? What part?"

"You know the one, a two-line walk-on in *Zombies' Revenge.* I know it's not a major role, but I will be on the big screen! True, no one will be able to recognize me in the ghoulish face makeup, but who cares? My name will be listed in the credits." She dragged him from the hall into her room. "It's going to happen. I told you it would happen."

Still thinking about the painful conversation he'd had with Bri's father, Ron managed a patient smile. "I am so happy for you, honey."

She tossed a handful of the clothing she'd discarded before going to the tryout onto the floor and flopped onto her unmade bed. "Not even a callback, mind you. I was hired on the spot!" She grabbed his hand and pulled him down on top of her. "Kiss me, you fool!"

He obliged. As their kisses intensified, he suddenly stopped and untangled himself from her grasp. "No, not like this. I can't do this. We promised to wait. I made a vow to you and to your father—"

She pulled him close once again. "Oh Ron, you're such a prude. I'll release you from your promise to me, and what Daddy doesn't know can't hurt him." She nuzzled Ron's neck. "Haven't you watched the action at our Saturday night parties? Sometimes I think you and I are the only virgins in the entire City of Angels." Her high-pitched laughter was brittle, like crackling glass. "I think it's time! It's not like we're strangers. We've been going together, whatever that means, since we were in middle school. I think it's time we grew up, don't you?"

When she tugged at his T-shirt, he leaped to his feet and turned toward the window overlooking the garage. Taking several deep breaths, he ran his fingers through his tousled hair. "Bri, I can't! This isn't how I pictured it happening." He heaved a massive sigh and lowered his body into a side chair beside the bed. "Keeping my word to both of us and to your father is important to me. Remember when we pledged to wait until our wedding day?"

Bri wrinkled her nose. "You sound like a monk out of the Dark Ages." After assuming what she hoped would be a provocative pose, she ran her tongue along her upper lip. "Maybe you don't love me enough." Her coo morphed into a pout. "Or maybe it's that you don't find girls attractive."

His eyes saddened at the barb; he flexed his jaw and slowly shook his head. "You know better than that."

"Fine!" She hopped off the bed and flounced her hair before the mirror above the dresser. "Just fine! You aren't the only fish in the pond, you know. Just this afternoon, one of the film's producers tried to take me to his trailer. I resisted, of course. Fortunately, a security guard came along, giving me time to escape. You should only know how many offers

I refuse at the parties I attend. Several a night, in fact." She flipped her hair behind one ear. "If you don't want me, I don't know how I'll respond the next time I'm propositioned."

"Bri, is this the life you really want? Becoming some balding, middle-aged man's momentary plaything?"

She clicked her tongue in frustration. "What I really want is you, Ron. But, I won't wait forever. If you don't want me, I'm sure I can find someone who does." She caught her reflection in the mirror over the dresser and smiled.

"I don't think you're ready to make a serious commitment right now."

"Don't be silly! I can't marry you just as my career is about to take off! It would be suicidal on all fronts."

"I agree," he admitted.

She clicked her tongue again. "Why do you always turn everything into a Supreme Court decision? I just want a little coming-of-age party to celebrate. Is that so terrible?"

For an instant, their eyes met and held. Color fused her cheeks. "Oh, forget it." She flounced out of the room into the hall. Slamming the door, Bri ran to catch up with Desiree and Mauri as they made their way down to the party.

"Come on, girl." Desiree grabbed Bri by the arm and dragged her toward the stairs. "So, you got the part. Wow! I'm impressed. That's great! The tequila is on you tonight. That's the custom here. Whenever you land a gig, you buy the drinks all around."

For an instant, the girl wondered how much the tab would be for the evening's libations. Running with this Malibu crowd was getting pretty expensive. But if that was what it took to make it in the entertainment world, Bri knew she would make the sacrifice. "Sounds good to me. Let's party!"

Swallowed by the deafening music, Bri failed to hear Summer Downy call to Ron from her open doorway. "Hey, Ronnie, I need your big, strong muscles to help me move my dresser to the far side of the room. Can you help me, pretty please?"

Bri's foot had barely hit the bottom step when someone thrust an icy, stemware glass of tequila into her hand and an all-too-familiar looking young man who always seemed to show up at their parties grasped her by the waist and began to gyrate to the music. Glancing over her shoulder, she hoped Ron was watching. But the stairwell remained empty. She shrugged and allowed herself to be swept into the festivities.

By the end of Bri's first week at the beach house, her inexperience with alcoholic beverages had given way to the pleasure of being temporarily free of what she'd begun calling her "small town inhibitions." It irked her that Ron continued to resist.

Tonight was her night, her time to celebrate. *And why shouldn't I celebrate?* she reasoned. While the role wasn't much—just two lines—it was a speaking part. Half the women at the party would die for the break she'd gotten that day. And after less than two months of standing in long lines at endless cattle calls, she'd landed a role at her first real audition.

Forget Ron, she told herself as she allowed another faceless guy to draw her into his arms and nuzzle her neck. *He's becoming such a party-pooper!*

For the next several hours, the tequila flowed. Shrieks of laughter and shouts above the ear-shattering music shook the rafters of the beach house. As the sun disappeared from the horizon, the partiers wandered down to the beach two by two. Bri's vision was blurred from the alcohol, yet she was still miffed at Ron for not attending her party. For a moment, she wondered where he'd been all evening.

An idea buzzed among the group about hopping a shuttle flight to a luxury resort in Cabo San Lucas for the weekend. *Mexico?* Bri grinned. *Today Mexico, tomorrow Monaco, or Paris. Yes, this is the way I want to live!*

Lost in her dreams of fame and fortune, the girl didn't hear Leo, her landlady Sam's special friend, step up behind her and blow on her neck. "Where's that boyfriend of yours?"

"He's pouting in his room!"

"Great! Come on, baby. Let me teach you how to party L.A.-style." He slipped his arm around her waist and whirled her about to face him. The sudden swirl unsettled her stomach for an instant. She glanced at the empty glass in her hand. *How many of these have I downed so far? And on an empty stomach!*

Her tongue felt thick and coated. She swallowed hard. "I–I need some salsa and chips." She staggered toward a snack table.

He took the empty glass from her hands and replaced it with one that was full. "There. That's all we need to really party."

Half carrying, half dragging her to a giant hammock at the far end of the deck, Leo set his drink on the deck and dropped them both into the swing. The glass of tequila slipped from her hand and spilled onto the wooden deck. Only half aware of her situation, she tried to push him away, but was no match for the man's superior weight and muscle strength. She protested, while he groaned with excitement. "Playing hard to get?" he growled. "I like that in my women."

Her vision blurred, she struggled to collect her wits about her. She felt him roll on top of her and trap her arms over her head with her tank top. From a long way off, she heard someone protesting, "No, no, not like this!"

"Come on, baby. You've been teasing me all night long," he repeated over and over as he buried his face in her neck.

The motion of the hammock after she had drunk several tequilas caused her empty stomach to revolt. Suddenly, in a panic, she clawed at his face and cried, "I think I'm going to be sick!"

The man froze for an instant. Genuine horror swept across his leering face.

"Leo, I'm going to be sick! Let me up!" She gulped and swallowed hard. "I mean it! I'm going to be sick!"

Leo struggled to leap to his feet. As a result, his frantic movements overturned the hammock onto the deck, causing Bri to land squarely onto his bare chest. Before he could break free, her upset stomach won the battle.

Mortified, Bri scrambled to her feet and tried to wipe the stench from her mouth. She stumbled inside the house and up the flight of stairs to her room. As she ripped her soiled top over her head and threw it on the floor, a knock sounded at the door. "Go away, Leo! Go away!"

It was Ron. "Bri? Are you all right?"

Relief flooded through her. "Pooh Bear! I'm so glad—" As she headed for the closed door, she caught a glimpse of her disheveled hair and makeup-streaked face in the mirror. "Wait! I'm not dressed!" She slipped into her swim robe, tied the sash about her waist and gargled a swig of mouthwash before opening the door. "Oh, Ronnie, I'm so glad to see you!" She threw herself into his arms.

Suddenly, she saw herself as he must see her and her tone changed. "What do you want? I'm sure you've already heard about my giant fiasco. Did you come to gloat over the fool I made of myself tonight?"

He stepped past her into the room. "Yes, I heard, but no, I didn't come to gloat. I just wanted to be certain you're OK. Are you OK?"

"No, I'm not OK!" she snapped between hiccups. "I may never be OK again!"

Realizing she needed time to sober up, he turned back toward the door. "I just wanted to tell you I called your dad this afternoon. He's packing up your clothes and sending everything in tomorrow's mail."

"What good will those old things do? I'll just look more like a country hick than I do already," she wailed.

"Hey, don't shoot the messenger. You asked me to call and I did. Next time you call, OK?"

Bri took several staccato breaths. "Did he say anything else?"

"Yes, he said to tell you that he loves you so very much and is praying for you."

"Oh." The girl's tone softened. "Is that all?"

"Pretty much. If you're feeling better, Summer and I are heading out for pizza. You're welcome to come along."

The thought of eating pizza sent her fleeing to the bathroom. Bri wasn't sure what upset her more, knowing that Ron was taking Summer out for pizza or the thought of eating pizza on her upset stomach. As she knelt before the porcelain god, the girl vowed she'd never drink again.

Taking advantage of her moment of weakness, Ron added, "Did you ever think that maybe your getting sick when you did was God's answer to your dad's prayer for protection?"

Too dizzy and too sick to protest, Bri groaned and crumbled into a heap on the ceramic tile floor as the bedroom door slammed. She believed her life was over. Not only had she embarrassed herself beyond words by getting sick in front of her friends, but she'd lost Ron to another woman.

"I'm sorry, Daddy. I just want to come home," she whimpered as she drifted into a troubled sleep. Dawn broke over the hills east of L.A. before Bri stirred. She ached all over as if one of her father's farm trucks had run her down and then backed up and done it again. Stumbling to her feet, she shed her soiled clothing and stepped into the shower. Her headache continued even as the cool water from the shower felt like gallons of water rushing over Niagara Falls, each drop like a tiny needle pricking her head, face, and body.

As she emerged from her bath, all was quiet in the beach house. The mariachi music had long since died. The partiers were either sleeping off their binges on sofas or on the floor, or they had gone home. Her empty stomach rumbled as she made her way down the stairs to the kitchen. Leaning over the breakfast bar, she found Sam. The woman turned as Bri entered the kitchen.

"I feel terrible," Bri began. "I'm so sorry. I made a fool of myself last night."

Sam laughed. "Hardly. We've all done it. You did what any neophyte would do after drinking too much booze on an empty stomach. Personally, I hope Leo learned a lesson—the jerk." The woman poured a cup of hot liquid. "Here, have a cup of herbal tea. This and a raw egg will settle your stomach."

"Raw egg?" Bri thought she'd lose whatever bile might have lingered in her stomach.

Sam laughed. "Drink the tea first. I was like you not so long ago. I remember trying so hard to fit into the L.A. scene. And now, I am the L.A. scene." She gave a snort. "Don't worry about Leo. He won't bother you again. Actually, I sent him packing this morning."

"Oh, I'm sorry, I—"

"Not because of last night, but because, frankly, I am tired of him mooching off of me." The woman grimaced. "They're all a bunch of moochers. By the way, did you say you were paying for all of us to spend next weekend in Cabo San Lucas?"

Bri shook her head. "I don't know."

"Well, that was the buzz this morning as people left the party. I can get us cheap tickets if you'd like," Sam volunteered. "It should be fun. Plus, I know a lot of movie producers and stars that frequent one particular resort. Would you like me to handle the reservations?"

"Uh, sure . . . thanks." As she sipped the hot tea, she wondered just how much the airfare and the expenses for a weekend at a resort in Mexico for twenty-plus people would cost. She wondered how she could get out of her promise, or if she reneged, how much credibility it might cost her.

The proposed weekend came and went, putting a giant hole in Bri's bank account. That she'd landed a second speaking role on the Thursday before the planned event helped assuage her nagging concern. That Ron refused to go irked her. Instead, he hopped a bus north to spend time with his mother who had fallen and broken her hip.

Bri's popularity continued to rise among her housemates as she funded shopping trips to Rodeo Drive and day cruises to Catalina. That she had become in demand for the escort service as a paid guest at sport celebrity parties added to her coffers. She'd also learned to keep her alcohol intake to a minimum so as not to make a fool of herself again. Agnes at the agency had warned her against drinking too much alcohol while on the clock. Girls who did so were immediately cut from the call list.

When Ron returned from visiting his mother following her hip surgery, he suggested, "I think we need to talk. Want to take a walk on the beach?"

"I'd like that. I really missed you while you were away."

They descended the steps down to the beach and headed north. Bri longed to take his hand, but hated to make the first move. "So, how did the movie shoot go?" he asked.

"It was so exciting! Of course, I did a lot of sitting around in costume in one hundred-degree weather, but just being a part of the action, wow! And I know this is only the beginning for me."

He kicked at a piece of driftwood left behind by the morning tide. Several seagulls swooped down hoping the two lone humans on the empty beach would feed them a few scraps. "Aren't you going to ask about my mother?"

She captured one of his hands in hers. "Of course. I was getting to that. How is she doing? Is she still in the hospital or have they let her go home yet?"

"She's home."

"I'm so glad."

She dipped her toes in the receding tide. When the water washed over her flip-flops, she giggled with delight. "Oh, Ronnie, isn't this place fabulous? Don't you just love the sand and the sun?" She released his hand and twirled in a circle, sending the skirt of her citrus print sundress billowing about her ankles.

He continued walking as she danced in the surf. When she reached for his hand, encouraging him to join her, he turned toward her. "In a week or so I plan to go back to make sure she's doing all right."

"Are you coming back?" She blinked in surprise.

He paused and shook his head. "I don't know, Bri. I've been spending my savings like water over Hoover Dam. My wallet is hurting."

She clicked her tongue and waved a dismissive hand. "I told you I'd give you some money."

"No, I won't let you do that. So far, I've floated my own boat down here and I don't intend to change that. What I need is to get a steady job—not just a supermarket promotional gig here and there—or go home." He turned toward the horizon and stuffed his hands in the pockets of his khaki cutoffs. "While your dad has been great to help out my mother, I need to step up, to help with the mounting medical bills. She's six months from being eligible for Medicare and her primary insurance only covers eighty percent of the outrageous hospital bill. As yet, no one knows how much the surgeon will charge. At this rate, she'll be in debt until her dying day."

Standing inches away from him, Bri nudged a broken shell with the toe of her sandal. "Sounds like you're giving up, quitting. Your mom's surgery, your depletion of cash—are they excuses to do what you've been aching to do since we first left home?"

He reached for her hands. She snatched them away. His arms fell to his side. "Bri, please try to understand. I have obligations. I can't play at being a movie star. It's time I man-up."

A chill ran through her body at the thought of being left alone. She resisted the urge to admit she might need him. She'd thought about his leaving every day since they'd arrived in L.A. Instead of being honest with herself or with him, her lip curled into a snarl. "Aw, come on. You've been planning to cut and run for some time now, haven't you?"

"Oh, Bri . . ." He hung his head and heaved a ragged sigh. "I'm sorry. I really have tried. And maybe if Mom hadn't fallen and broken her hip, I could have made it."

"Go ahead—just go ahead and leave. So what if you promised my father you'd take care of me."

"When I explained my situation to your father, he released me from that promise. He urged me to do what I believed to be right."

"And what about me?"

"He wants me to urge you to come home, too, though neither of us really thought you'd listen."

"You're right about that." She threw her hand up in the air. "It's OK, really. Let's face it. You don't fit in with my friends anyway. I'm not sure you and I are on the same page anymore. We don't even speak the same language any longer."

"Our lives do seem to be going totally different directions." He reached for her hand again and she yanked it away. "Bri, I still love you with my whole heart, but I can't stand watching you change from the sweet girl I grew up with into a party girl I really don't know."

"Party girl? Speaking of party girls, is Summer going with you?"

"Of course not. Where did that come from?"

"Oh, I've seen the way she looked at you before you left, all googly eyed. And now that you're back, I figured you'd want to take her home to meet your mama."

Ron's eyes narrowed. "That crack is beneath you, Bri."

The young woman shrugged off his censure. "Dare I ask what you are going to do with yourself stuck in the valley? Work in the orange groves with my dad?"

"That's exactly what I plan to do, at least until next semester when I can enroll in the police academy. He's asked me to lead a team of workers." He stuffed his hands in his pockets. "I really hate leaving you alone here in L.A."

"Don't flatter yourself, Ron, I'll be just fine without you, maybe better than fine. I've learned to 'fly solo' while you've been gone."

"Exactly what does that mean?"

She flipped her long blond locks from her neck. "I am no longer the naive little innocent you left behind. I can take care of myself. By the way, the gang is all heading to Mexico again this weekend. Wanna come along?"

"Let me guess. You're picking up the tab, right? I see the way your so-called friends are mooching off of you. When you run out of money, they'll run out on you."

"That's ludicrous! You think you know so much. I don't believe you. You're such a stick-in-the-mud. You won't allow yourself to loosen up and enjoy life!" She clenched her teeth together. Her lips tightened into a thin, disapproving line.

Without another word, he turned and trudged back toward the beach house.

"I never thought you were such a quitter, Ron Chaney!" she shouted over the roar of the surf. "And don't bother to call to find out how I'm doing. You can tell my dad the same thing. I'll throw my phone into the surf if you do."

Kicking at the salt water splashing her toes, she resisted the almost overwhelming urge to run after him and beg him to stay. Instead, she stared out at the horizon. *If that's the way things are, then that's the way things are. I can make it on my own!* When Ron mentioned money, he touched a sore nerve. Bri also fretted over her depleting finances. Her bank account was worse off than Ron could imagine. She knew she'd become an easy "touch" to those she called her friends, but she argued that that was the price of doing business in Hollywood. *Schmoozing and networking cost money,* she reasoned. *I'll call Sabrina at the escort service right after checking in with Agnes at the agency. I refuse to go home like a whipped puppy with my tail between my legs! I won't do that—ever!*

CHAPTER ELEVEN

Admitting Defeat

Ron sat in the straight-back oak chair across the desk from Bri's father, his head in his hands. "I'm sorry, sir. I tried to reason with her but I failed. I shouldn't have mentioned her so-called friends."

Bob folded his hands on the cluttered desktop and listened while the younger man recited his morning conversation with the beloved Brianna. "I tried to point out to her that her so-called friends are bleeding her dry. She took several of the girls shopping on Rodeo Drive and paid for everything, even matching diamond friendship bracelets from Tiffany's."

"But you said she has a part in a movie." The older man held out hope.

"Right! A classic B movie that will go straight into the DVD rental market instead of into the theater! It's better than nothing, I guess. Most evenings she attends parties for hire, to pretty up the place, as she calls it. But my main worry is her drinking. She drinks when she's happy; she drinks when she's sad; she drinks with her friends as well as alone."

He hesitated before asking, "Is she into drugs as well?"

"Not that I know of, but I've not been her confidant of late." His words came out in a hiccup. "There was a time when she couldn't wait to regale me with every moment of her day. I'm afraid those days are gone forever."

"For me too." Tears glistened in the father's eyes and a sigh escaped his lips. "You tried your best. I'm sure you did all you could, son."

"No, I didn't, sir. There must have been something else I could have said or done, short of hog-tying her to the hood of her Miata. I let her get my goat."

Bob smiled at the imagery of Bri being tied to the hood like a deer bagged on a hunt. "No, no, there was little you could do. How many times over the years since her mama died have I let Honey Bee 'get my goat,' as you put it? She's a headstrong young woman, Ron. I doubt anyone could change her mind once it is set. Obviously, I failed the day she left for L.A. I should have done something to stop her."

The young man shook his head and wiped his nose on his shirtsleeve. "Maybe I should have stayed . . ."

"You don't believe that. You have an obligation to your mother. I'm sorry, but she needs you more than my wayward daughter does. And frankly, it's time for you to begin working toward your goals instead of trying to live out my daughter's dreams."

"Yes, sir."

"And that includes dating other women. I hate to say it, but you can't wait for her to come to her senses." He cast a wistful glance toward the hallway. "Maybe I should try to call her . . ."

"I wouldn't advise that, sir," Ron cautioned. "She threatened to change her phone number or throw her cell phone into the surf if you or I tried to call."

Again, the older man shook his head sadly. "Talk about burning bridges . . ."

"I know, sir. I hope you still need me in the orchards."

"Absolutely. You'll be reporting early tomorrow morning? I've told Bette to expect you. And, don't let her rag on you about Bri. I love my older daughter, but she can be a bit of a nag at times." Bob rose out of his chair and extended his hand.

Ron grinned. "I remember. Thank you again, sir, for giving me a job right now. As for my goals, they'll stay on hold until I can get my mother's financial affairs in order."

"Don't wait too long. Life has a way of detouring one's best intentions." Before releasing Ron's hand, Bob added, "Let me know how it's going for you and for your mom. I know it's too late for the fall term at the police academy, but you should apply for the winter term."

When Ron started to object, the older man lifted one hand to silence him. "Don't say it. Your entrance fee has been paid, along with your first semester at the academy. After all you did for my daughter, I wanted to do this for you. I believe in you, son. You are made of tough stuff. You will make a great policeman."

"Sir! I can't allow you to—"

"Don't let your stupid pride get in the way, dear boy. And never look a gift horse in the mouth!" Bob chuckled. "Besides, I know a good investment when I see one."

"Yes, sir. I won't let you down."

"I know you won't, son. Seven o'clock tomorrow morning, right?"

"Yes, sir!" Ron gave a snappy salute, turned, and exited the office.

Bob sank back into his chair. His breath caught in his throat; his heart literally ached within his chest. He'd never before experienced such pain, even with the loss of Angie. With Angie's death, he knew it was over, final—no more pain or suffering for her. She would rest safely in the arms of Jesus until the resurrection morning. But with Bri, he imagined that his pain was only beginning.

He sat lost in thought for some time. Outside the office window, the shadows of evening gathered on the lawn. Nightmarish visions of his beloved daughter trapped in a very real web of evil swirled through his brain. If only he could go to L.A. to see her, to talk with her. If only he could hear her voice again. If only . . .

CHAPTER TWELVE

Life on the Streets

Bri ambled along the water's edge. Waves of self-pity, self-destruction, and then self-aggrandizement pummeled her brain. Her emotions were ever changing. As she neared the steps to the beach house, Sam called to her from the deck. "Hey, Bri, are you busy tonight?"

Bri shook her head no.

Sam met her at the top of the stairs. "I accidentally double-booked two parties tonight, an escort assignment at an NBA star's bash and a birthday celebration for a producer's wife. Obviously, I'm going to the producer's. Who knows what kinds of leads I can get hobnobbing with Hollywood's rich and famous? Maybe a movie role! Can you take the sports gig for me?"

"Sure. What time do I need to be there?" Bri managed a smile.

"In time for the happy hour, around seven, I would think. It's a dress-to-the-hilt event. All you have to do is be glamorous, or as Hedy Lamarr said, 'To be glamorous, just stand still and look stupid.' "

"Right. Thanks for asking me. You sure do quote that woman often enough. I need a diversion tonight. But first I need a drink."

"She was a wise woman in the ways of Hollywood." Sam handed her an ice-cold can of beer. "Hey, are you all right? You look terrible. Are you sure you're up to a party tonight?"

She took the can from Sam's hand and sipped the cold liquid. "I will be. This will help."

"Be careful, girl. Don't drink too much. You know the agency doesn't want their girls drunk at these events."

Bri snorted, "Yes, mama."

The older woman slipped an arm around the girl. "Hey, I'm more like an older sister than a mother."

Bri flopped onto the end of a white leather sectional sofa. Sand filtered from her flip-flops onto the dark-stained hardwood floor. She put her bare feet on the nearby white leather ottoman.

A frown formed on Sam's face. She stood behind the sofa, out of Bri's peripheral vision. "Ron came to see me. He paid the rest of last month's rent before he left. I'm so sorry. Men! You can't live with them and you can't live without them! What a bummer."

That another suntanned, beefy guy named Jerry had moved in with Sam a day after Leo left only punctuated Sam's remarks. Jerry also seemed motivated to "make it" in the movie business. Both men showed about as much initiative as a slug on a rainy day in Oregon. For a moment, Bri questioned her landlady's taste in men. *Will poor Sam go through life falling for one loser after another?* she wondered. *At least Ron has gumption, even if he is the most infuriating male ever!*

As Bri tried to decide between wearing her new thigh-high, ebony-sequined strapless dress and her red satin, floor-length number, she wondered if her father was on his way down to drag her home. *It would be just like him to think he can bully me into submission!* She smiled to herself. *If he is, he's in for a big surprise. I won't be here. I'll warn Sam not to tell him where I am either.*

After slathering her face with several layers of creams and cosmetics, she studied the results in the mirror. *There! Tonight I need black sequins and a heavy swatch of blush to erase all traces of swollen eyes from my face!* Yet even with extra-thick, smoky-gray eye shadow, she couldn't miss the haunting look in her sullen blue eyes. Determined to have fun regardless of the less-than-stellar day she'd experienced, Bri carefully applied bright red lipstick and smacked her lips together. "Look out Hollywood! With one swipe of passion red lipstick, this country hick from the Central Valley orange groves has evolved into a true woman of the world!"

*****

Bri paused outside the gates of the famous basketball star's estate at precisely 7:00 P.M. She sighed with relief that she'd made it on time through the early evening traffic. A uniformed guard asked to see her invitation and then waved her on to the main house, an opulent structure that sprawled in several directions like the tentacles of a giant squid. A uniformed valet met her at the front entrance, checked her invitation, and relieved her of her keys while another equally stuffy gentleman held the giant carved wooden double doors open for her to enter the foyer. Mirrors wrapped the room from head to toe. Even the glossy Venetian tile on the floor sparkled in the light reflected from the oversized chandelier hanging from the forty-foot ceiling. *It's like stepping inside a giant fluorescent tube,* she thought as a uniformed man she perceived to be the butler asked again to see her invitation at the door.

For a moment she froze. From somewhere beyond the portico, a space large enough to swallow an average-sized home in the valley without burping, a live rock band syncopated their deafening music with the staccato of loud voices, ice clinking against crystal, and riotous laughter as if the level of noise they made indicated how much fun everyone was having.

Since coming to L.A., she'd attended six or seven such parties as a pretty face and a paid, convivial guest, but this night, she suddenly felt out of her league. *Who am I kidding? I don't belong here.* She stiffened her spine. *You can do this, girl!* The butler gestured toward the room beyond the foyer. His condescending smile indicated he'd read her mind. Taking a deep breath, she lifted her chin and tugged at the hem of her thigh-high skirt. Her stilettos clicked on the highly polished marble as she strolled in the direction indicated.

For dozens, the party had long-since begun. With one sweep of the room, she recognized the faces of several sports and television stars. A waiter carrying a silver tray of drinks placed a filled crystal champagne glass in her shaking hands. *You can do this! This is what your dream is all about. Someday you will be living in digs like this and throwing outrageous parties for your friends. And maybe hiring great-looking guys to "pretty up" the place.* She took a sip of the cold beverage and felt the tingle on her tongue followed by immediate warmth soothing her quaking nerves. *Ooh, I really needed that!*

She took a second sip, inhaled slowly, pasted on a confident smile, and weaved her way through the dancing couples toward a group of partiers surrounding someone whom she identified as the host due to his extraordinary height and the forced laughter of his fawning guests. Remaining on the outskirts of the clique, she gazed about the room.

The parlor gave new meaning to the term "great room." Short of the visit to the rotunda of the U.S. Capitol on her eighth-grade field trip, it was the largest room she'd ever seen. And the main attraction was beyond the four walls—the Pacific Ocean. At each end of the space, massive sliding glass doors pocketed one another, virtually disappearing from view when opened.

She'd barely taken another sip from her glass when a waiter placed a fresh one in her hand. "No, no, I—"

"Aw, don't be a party pooper, little lovely," a male voice with a thick British accent whispered in her ear. He slipped his arm around her waist and turned her about to face him. "Come dance with me."

Remembering the famous Hedy Lamarr's wisdom about glamorous women, she widened her smile and eased into his arms. The music shifted to an easy "made for intimate dancing" number. As he tightened his arms about her, she glanced appreciatively at her dance partner's chiseled profile and patrician nose. "So, what brings you to these parts?" he whispered. "Don't tell me you're one of old Marvin's conquests, are you?"

"Marvin?"

"Marvin, our host. Marvin is his given name. His glitzier name is his public name, the one his female fans swoon over. I know old Marv from high school in Pittsburgh."

She smiled up at him. "You went to school in Pittsburgh? I would have guessed Eton or Oxford."

"No. I grew up in Waterford, England, the son of a duke, but my folks split when I was eleven and I moved to western Pennsylvania with my mother. So, are you one of Marvin's conquests?"

"No, I'm here to pretty up the party."

"Well, you certainly do that." His wide grin revealed a full array of glistening white teeth. She couldn't contain her grin when the theme song of *Jaws* wafted through her brain.

"What's so funny?"

She shook her head. "Nothing really. I guess I can't imagine a suave gentleman like you growing up in the wilds of Pennsylvania."

"It was burdensome at times. Want to stroll out onto the deck and watch the sunset? I need a cigarette and old Marvin's current skirt won't let me smoke inside."

Remembering her last adventure on a similar deck, she begged off. The Englishman shrugged and left. Left to her own devices, Bri wandered to the marble-topped bar and sat down on an available stool. Setting her empty glass down, she watched the action through the giant silver-lined mirror behind the hand-carved chestnut bar.

It was through the mirror that she first noticed a tall, good-looking man of about thirty, with blond surfer's hair and a wicked smile, watching her from the deck. Their eyes met. She looked away. When she glanced back, he was gone. Turning quickly, she found herself facing the third pearl button on his expensive silk pleated shirt.

"Hi, I'm Tom. I play center for the Palm Springs Wranglers. Where have you been all my life, pretty lady?"

Not being a basketball fan, Bri widened her most practiced smile and ran her hand along the left lapel of his tux. "*Ooh,* how impressive."

"No name?" The man was almost drooling on her bare shoulders.

"Bri, Brianna Marie."

"What are you drinking, Brianna Marie?" He signaled for the bartender.

"Sorry, I've had plenty already. Gotta drive home, you know. Don't want a DUI." She winked and flashed him an even wider grin.

He bent down and whispered in her ear, "If you play your cards right, little girl, you won't need to go home tonight."

Before she could reply, the bartender appeared. "What will you be having, Tom?"

"I'd like a double bourbon. The same for the lady."

"Oh, no, I couldn't. I don't handle my drinks well," she warned.

A glint of pleasure flashed in his eyes. "Nonsense! The only way to overcome that is to drink more."

When the bartender returned with the two drinks, she pushed hers aside and said, "I'd like a diet Pepsi with lots of ice, please."

The bartender eyed Tom questioningly. Tom shrugged. "Give the lady whatever she wants. Your loss, sweetie! Old Marv stocks only the best Kentucky bourbon in the nation."

She glanced around the room searching for an escape from Tom, whom she had already nicknamed "the lecher." The bartender returned with her soda. Tom intercepted the glass. Before handing the frosty glass to her, he pointed toward their host. "What a guy! He's having too much fun. Your soda, my dear."

"Thank you." She beamed up at him. "So where do you call home?"

"I'm a dyed-in-the-wool Santa Monica beach bum." He laughed. He pointed at the soda in her glass. "Aren't you going to drink that thing?"

She took a sip. The soda tasted a little off, as if it had too much syrup in it and not enough fizz. "What do you do when you aren't bumming off the Santa Monica pier?"

"Absolutely nothing. My daddy died and left me enough money for three lives, even by L.A. standards. I'm stinkin' rich!"

The man's boast startled Bri. Her displeasure must have registered on her face because he threw back his head and laughed. "You are so naive, little girl. What pumpkin patch did you crawl out from under? Money runs this town. If you have it, you can get anything you want—fame, power, booze, drugs, sex . . ."

Somewhere after his declaration that money ran the town, she began to feel dizzy. Her sight blurred. Bri could feel a headache coming on. "Please excuse me, Tom. I don't feel so well." When she tried to stand up, her feet felt as if they were encased in concrete. She stumbled.

"Take another sip of soda. It might help."

She did as told, but instead of feeling better, she felt dizzier. She grabbed hold of the marble-topped bar with one hand to steady herself and held her forehead with the other.

"Here, let me help you, little girl." He slid an arm protectively about her waist and drew her close to his side. "Perhaps you should lie down until you feel better."

"No, no, I–I–I don't want to . . ." Bri shook her head, but his hold about her waist intensified. Something definitely wasn't right. Warning bells jangled in her brain. "Did you slip something into my . . ." Panicked, she tried to call out for someone to help her, but an uninvited giggle erupted from her throat instead.

Tom guided the stumbling young woman through the crowd of partiers. "A little too much to drink," Tom murmured to concerned individuals as they passed by. "Can't hold her liquor," he told others. In her ear, he soothed, "Just rest your head on my shoulder, sweetie. You'll be OK; I promise."

At the base of the stairs leading to the second floor of the mansion, her world went black. She sank to the floor. The last Bri could recall was Tom scooping her into his arms. Wild and crazy dreams surfaced in her mind and then floated away. Her cries for help came out as whimpers. She saw her father's face, filled with concern. "Oh, Daddy, help me!" She reached out to him but he instantly faded from view with the promise, "I'm praying for you, Honey Bee." His words drifted away like foam on the surface of the ebbing tide.

Hours later, Bri stirred and opened her eyes. She found herself in an unfamiliar bedroom. A security light filtered through palm fronds from outside the room danced on the floor and bed. Her head pounded; her arms felt heavy, as if being held down by an unseen force. She fought to focus her dazed mind on her situation. *What happened? Where am I? What am I doing here?*

As she struggled to sit up, the silken sheet covering her body fell away, revealing her state of undress. The sequined dress, along with her underclothing, lay scattered about the thick white carpet beside the bed. Trembling, she fumbled with the switch on the lamp on the nightstand.

The small halo of light from the lamp illuminated a large room swathed in white satin—white satin sheets, pillowcases, and padded headboard. A white velvet settee and two baby blue high-back upholstered boudoir chairs occupied one corner of the room. A white triple dresser with a large wall mirror filled the other.

Beyond the room, a vacuum cleaner purred. She could hear people chatting in Spanish in the hallway. Pain coursed through her when she shook her head, attempting to dislodge the confusion.

"Party. I was at a party," she mumbled. "I was hired to work the room. I had a diet drink, but then what?" Slowly, she reconstructed the events of the night before. "There was a man, a beach bum, so he called himself— Tom, I think." When she tried to stand, her legs wobbled like a newborn calf. She fell back onto the edge of the bed. That's when the full impact of what had happened hit her. "No! No! It can't be! Oh, Ron, I'm so sorry. I've got to get home!" Her wail fell on deaf ears.

Distraught, she managed to dress and stumble down the stairs. "My car! Where's my car?" she shouted.

The disinterested help glanced her way as she passed. One older woman shouted something and the butler appeared at the foot of the stairs. He took her arm and guided her down the last of the stairs, through the foyer, and to her car. As he opened the door to the Miata for her, he reprimanded her for drinking too much. "Are you sure you're sober enough to drive home?" he asked.

"Yes, yes, I just want to get out of here. I've got to go home."

Reluctantly, the butler handed her the keys to her car.

"Wait! Wait!" A woman, wearing a gray-and-white maid's uniform, dashed across the lawn to the car. "Your purse. You forgot your purse, Miss."

Sympathy emanated from the woman's eyes as she handed Bri the tiny sequin-covered, compact-size purse, which contained her bank card, credit cards, driver's license, Social Security card, cell phone, and a spare tube of lipstick. "Oh, thank you," the girl clutched the purse to her chest. "My entire life is in here."

Bri climbed into the car and inserted the key into the ignition. The vehicle roared to life. After revving the engine a few times, she glanced up at the concerned man and woman standing nearby. Both looked worried for her. "I'm fine. See! I'm fine."

She eased the car down the long driveway, past the security gates, and onto the canyon road leading to Malibu. As the car clicked off the miles, she regained her wits about her; memories of the previous night returned. She had no doubt that she'd been drugged and raped. Anger welled up inside her, wrestling with a slew of vain regrets. The morning breeze whipped her tangled curls about her makeup-streaked face. Tears tumbled down her cheeks.

With the full impact of what had happened to her the previous night, new worries emerged. *What if I become pregnant or contract some terrible STD?* She'd seen enough TV shows to know she should head to the nearest hospital and report the crime. She ached to go back to the beach house and take a very long shower. Glancing at the purse laying on the seat beside her, she longed to call Ron or her father but couldn't bring herself to do so. The thought of admitting to Ron, and especially her father, what had happened to her was beyond mortifying. *A shower! That's what I need!* She stepped on the gas, turned away from the street leading to the closest hospital, and headed toward the beach house.

The unmistakable wail of a police siren startled her. In her haste, she'd run a stop sign on the last corner. "No! Not now!" She pulled onto the side of the road and stopped. A tall, angular policewoman strode toward her car. Tears streamed down Bri's face. She buried her face in her hands on the wheel.

"Miss, you failed to come to a complete stop at the corner. May I see your registration and driver's license, please?"

"Yes, sir, um, ma'am," she sniffed and opened her glove compartment for the auto registration. Handing the sheet of paper to the sober-faced policewoman, she reached for her wallet and pressed the clasp. The purse popped open—empty! Even her lipstick was missing. She gazed pleadingly at the officer. "Everything is gone. Someone stole my license and my credit cards!"

The officer spoke into a microphone attached to her collar. "I need a check on license plate number . . ."

Confused, Bri waited for the officer to finish speaking to dispatch. "Honest! Someone stole my ID cards and even my cell phone!"

Instead, the officer drew her gun and pointed it at Bri. "Please step out of the car with your hands on your head, Miss."

Bri obeyed, but as she did, she wobbled.

"Have you been drinking, Miss? Or are you on drugs?"

The girl steadied herself against the car's rear fender. "No, no! Not since last night when I was raped."

The officer asked Bri to walk a straight line. When she weaved from one side to the other, she was given a Breathalyzer test. Though her blood alcohol level registered within the appropriate limits, she staggered as if on something.

The officer's eyes shifted for a moment and then resumed their cold, emotionless stare. "Turn around and place the palms of your hands on the car. I'm taking you in for a blood test to see what drug you're on."

"But I . . ."

As the policewoman read Bri her rights, the girl felt as if she were trapped in a nightmarish TV police drama. Shackled and tossed into the rear seat of the patrol car, she couldn't contain herself any longer. She cried as if her heart would break. Someone had not only stolen her virginity, but also her driver's license, bank card, credit cards, her Social Security card, and her cell phone.

"My name is Brianna Austin. I am an actress. I live at . . ." Determined to maintain a semblance of self-control, she repeated her personal information to a second and then a third doubting L.A. city policeman. "An actress," he snorted. "Isn't everyone?"

Bri sighed. "Do I get to make a phone call?"

"After we finish processing you," the aging officer replied. "Face the camera. *[Flash]* Turn left. *[Flash]* Turn right. *[Flash]*."

If she'd been embarrassed by the idea of a hospital exam, it was nothing compared to the search another policewoman gave her. "Is anyone going to do anything about my rapist or the person who stole my credit cards and license?" No one cared to hear the terrible details about the events of the night before.

After what seemed like an endless round of questions and inquiries, Bri found herself face to face with her one phone call. Would it be to her father or to Ron? Too mortified to call her father or Ron, she called Sam. After Bri poured out her story to her landlady, Sam agreed to post bail.

By the time the officers processed Bri, it was too late in the afternoon for her arraignment. "What's going to happen to me?" she asked a balding, pockmarked-face desk clerk.

"You'll spend the night in lockup," the man admitted.

"In jail?" Bri gasped.

"Afraid so, Miss. Don't worry. The judge will get to hearing your case as soon as possible tomorrow morning."

She and a younger female police officer walked past cell after cell crowded with miscreants of all shapes and sizes. The police officer stopped and unlocked the door to the last cell on the right. She removed Bri's handcuffs and told her to step inside. As the iron-barred door clanged shut behind her, Bri's eyes adjusted to the darkness and she saw several pairs of eyes staring back at her. Not knowing where to go or what to say, she sat down on an empty space on a long bench bolted to the back wall. "You can't sit there. That's Myra's place!" a voice snarled.

Bri rose and moved to another empty spot on the bench.

"No! You can't sit there either. That's Carmen's place," the same voice snarled.

Again, the terrified Bri rose and glanced around the small, darkened room. By now her eyes had adjusted to the cell's dimmer light. Seven women occupied a space meant for no more than four. By their heavy makeup and cheaply made clothing, she guessed that three of the women were prostitutes, while two looked as if they'd just been in a brawl. One had a recently treated cut on her face and the other had a black eye and swollen cheek. Bri guessed that the last two were homeless by their disheveled clothing and by the strong odor of perspiration. The woman who'd refused her a place to sit sauntered over to where the uncertain Bri stood.

"So what are you in for, girlie? Stealing some john's wallet?"

Bri blinked in surprise.

"Leave the kid alone, Maisie." The second woman whom Bri suspected of being arrested for fighting pushed the first woman aside. "Don't judge her by your standards." Taking Bri by the arm, she led her to the far end of the bench. "Come on over here, sweetie. I'll protect you."

"Huh!" Maisie snorted. "You're the one the poor girl needs protectin' from."

"Aw, shut your trap," the woman with the black eye hissed.

Before the two women could take their altercation further, a policewoman unlocked the cell door and called to the two women. "Judge is ready to see you two—again!"

"Aw, cutie, you know you live to see us again," Maisie chortled.

As they disappeared down the corridor, one of the women Bri assumed was arrested for prostitution waved to her. "Come on over and sit yourself down. My name is Yvette. It's going to be a long night. So, what's your name, sweetie?"

Shaken by all the events of the last twenty-four hours, the kindness in Yvette's voice broke through Bri's studied composure. Tears brimmed in the frightened girl's eyes. She rubbed away the last streaks of mascara staining her cheeks.

"So what happened that caused a nice girl like you to wind up in a stink hole like this?" The woman sat down beside her and took Bri's quivering hand in hers. "Stop shaking. You're safe. I promise. You can trust me. No one's going to hurt you, I promise."

At the moment, Bri doubted she could trust anyone ever again. But she needed to tell her tale to someone, anyone, even a streetwalker named Yvette. What started in short spurts of information grew into a deluge of painful words and sobs from Bri. Her story held the other prisoners spellbound.

As she told them about her triumph in the local production of *Beauty and the Beast* and her dream to make it big in Hollywood, the women in the cell nodded and mumbled. They'd all shared the same vision of hope. And with slight variations, they'd all been brought down by the hard reality of life in the big city and by slime like Tom, the beach bum.

"So what are you in for?" Yvette asked.

"I'm charged with running a stop sign and failing a drug test."

"A DUI. That's serious business in L.A. County," Yvette admitted.

"But I was drugged and raped! Doesn't anybody care about that?"

"Probably not. Outside of the drugs, sex is part of the package in Hollywood," Yvette snorted. "Do you know what kind of drug the creep slipped into your drink?"

Bri shook her head.

Yvette clicked her tongue. "Could be just about anything. Date rape drugs are as varied as their users."

"When I leave here, I don't know what to do or where to go," Bri sniffed.

"If you can, go home to your dad," a redheaded woman named Dana advised.

A bleached blond named Gabi stepped out of the shadows. "Go home before this life consumes everything that is good in you. Take it from me; it will eat you up from the inside out."

For the next few hours, each of the women in the cell told her story. While the details varied, each ended the same. When the lights dimmed in the hallway, Yvette advised, "We'd better get some sleep. Arraignment court starts early."

Bri's stomach growled. "Don't they feed you around here?"

Yvette laughed. "Sorry, honey. You missed the slop they call dinner by ten minutes."

"It wasn't so bad tonight. The powdered mashed potatoes were almost edible," a woman called Nina admitted. "I'm not so sure about the gray string beans though. They dared you to eat them."

"Oh, well. I've dieted before." Bri laughed.

"Hey, Bri," Dana volunteered, "I didn't eat the stale brownie they brought for dessert. You can have it if you'd like."

"Really? Thanks." Eagerly, the girl reached for it. As she did, their hands touched; their eyes met. A wave of compassion passed between them. Dana knew and understood her plight firsthand.

During the long night, Bri tossed and turned on the lumpy mattress pulled out from the wall. As she stared into the darkness of the cell, she could hear her cellmates whimper in their sleep, mumble unintelligible words, and occasionally cry out. She'd finally fallen asleep when she felt Dana shake her shoulder. "Bri," the woman whispered, "You've been talking in your sleep."

"Oh, sorry," Bri mumbled.

"It's OK. We all do sometimes. Go back to sleep if you can."

Bri turned her face toward the wall and closed her eyes only to see Tom's leering grin. Her hips ached from sleeping on a lumpy mattress on the concrete floor. She awoke to the unpleasant sounds of her cellmates coughing, wheezing, and relieving themselves in the corner facility. She'd barely gathered her wits about her when their jailer served a breakfast of sticky oatmeal, a cup of powdered milk, coffee, and an orange. *Hardly the meal being served at my daddy's table,* she silently mused.

After the metal trays were removed, another police officer returned and began calling out the names of the women for their arraignments. As Dana's name was called, the woman handed her a paper napkin on which a street address was written. Bri recognized the street to be in East L.A. "If worse comes to worse, look me up," Dana whispered.

CHAPTER THIRTEEN

Reasoning Against Reason

The jangle of the telephone broke Bob's concentration. He glanced up from the stack of papers he was signing. "Bette, can you get that? It's probably the water commissioner in Sacramento. He promised to call me with the results of this morning's vote."

Bette spoke in low tones for a few moments. "Daddy," she handed the receiver to her father. "It's Jason Toomey, our attorney. He says it's urgent that he speak with you."

The tired businessman groaned and scratched his grizzled face. "What's gone wrong with the Foot Hill negotiations now? I swear those guys are more changeable than the weather in Omaha." He placed the receiver up to his ear. "Hello? Jason? How can I help you this morning?"

All color drained from Bob's face as he listened to the family attorney on the other end of the phone. Barely audible monosyllables punctuated Bob's stunned silence. He gulped several times, as if to catch his breath.

"What is it, Daddy?" Bette asked from across the room.

Bob covered the speaker end of the receiver with one hand. "It's your sister. She's been arrested and is being arraigned for a DUI in the L.A. County courthouse this morning."

He again spoke into the telephone. "Yes, yes, please send in one of your L.A. attorneys to represent her. Yes, I understand. Of course, anything you can do will be much appreciated."

Bette stared as her father completed his conversation with the family attorney. Bob hung up the phone and leaped to his feet as a fist pounded on the door, rattling it off its hinges. Before either he or Bette could answer it, Ron burst into the room.

"Sir! Something awful has happened. I just heard from Sam, Bri's landlady. Bri has been arrested for driving under the influence. It seems she attended a party where someone slipped a date rape drug into her drink. She passed out and when she awoke, she realized she'd been, uh, raped." The younger man swiped a distracted hand through his short-cropped hair.

"My baby! My poor baby . . ."

Bob fell back in his chair as Ron continued. "On her way to the beach house, a cop stopped her for running a stop sign. When she tried to give the officer her license, she discovered her ID, credit cards, bank card, cell phone, her entire identity was missing from her purse."

"Bette, cancel your sister's credit cards immediately! You know the ones. Call Fred at the bank and put him on alert for any movement on her accounts," Bob shouted. His hands trembled; his voice broke with emotion.

Bette whipped out her cell phone and began to carry out his directions. Bob turned back to Ron. "What else? Has she been arraigned?"

"Yes, Sam called me and said she covered Bri's bail so she could be released. The judge set her bail at ten thousand dollars. Bri gave Sam the title for the Miata until she could sort everything out. It seems that whoever stole Bri's credit cards also emptied her bank account."

"That's it! Bette, take over the negotiations for the land purchase. Hold them off. Tell them we've had a family emergency. They'll understand. I'm driving to L.A. right now."

"You can't!" Ron grabbed the man's arm. "You can't go down there."

"You and what army is going to stop me?" His eyes flashed with fury.

"Sir! After her release from jail this morning, Bri left the beach house.

She took a small suitcase of her clothes with her and didn't give Sam a forwarding address. That's why Sam called me. She wanted to know where to send the rest of Bri's belongings. Sam hasn't a clue as to where she went. Bri just called a taxi and left." Ron could barely contain his anxiety. "Don't you think I would be halfway to L.A. by now if I had any idea where to go once I arrived?"

Bob's face turned beet red; his blood pressure appeared to be heading off the charts. Fearful he'd have a stroke, Bette whipped around the desk and massaged his shoulders. "It's OK, Daddy. It's going to be OK. You know Brianna. She'll be all right. She always lands on her feet."

"Bette, what did Fred at the bank say?" he asked.

"He's put a hold on all of her credit cards. The thief will be tagged the instant she or he tries to use them. But whoever stole them has a day's head start. The last charge of twenty-five hundred dollars was made at an expensive jewelry store in Las Vegas. Unfortunately, the way Bri's been spending money of late, no one at the bank detected the theft in time to stop it."

Bob pounded his fist on the desktop. The frame containing his wife's photo collapsed onto the desk. "I've got to do something, anything."

"It's only money, Daddy. Isn't that what you always say? It's only money?" Bette soothed.

Bob wouldn't be consoled. He ran his fingers through his thinning gray hair and pounded his fist on the desktop a second time. "I don't care about the money. I want my daughter back!"

"I know," she cooed. "I know."

Suddenly, he leaped to his feet, startling both Ron and Bette. "Well I can't just sit by and wait for a call from the police saying they found a woman's body beneath some freeway overpass and they think it's my daughter. I've got to do something!"

Ron tried to reason with the distraught father. "What can you do, sir? Obviously, Bri's gone into hiding somewhere; probably planning to jump bail, if I know her. If anything, your daughter is clever. If she doesn't want to be found, she won't be."

"Why didn't she call me? She knows I love her. If she'd asked, I would have rushed to her aid. My beautiful Honey Bee, where are you?"

Bette hugged her father about the neck. "Bri's obviously embarrassed, Daddy. You know she has enormous pride. Remember the time she backed that bulldozer into a tree trunk? She can't admit failure to you."

"She's right, sir. Your daughter has a whale of a lot of pride," Ron added. "If you wish, I'll go down and try to retrace her steps. But I'll warn you, she told me many times that if you or anyone else comes looking for her, she'll run and we'll never see her again."

Bob stormed over to the window and stared out at orange groves across the road. "No, I can't let you do that, Ron. Your mother needs you. As you know, her hip isn't healing properly and she's in a lot of pain." He exhaled in defeat. "And you're right. Bri told me the same thing. But that won't stop me from hiring a private investigator to track her down."

"You'd better warn him to keep a low profile," Ron cautioned. "I'd hate to think what she'll do if she discovers you are having her followed."

"And what will you do if he finds her?" Bette interjected. "Drag her home by the hair on her head?"

"Just knowing she's alive and well will be enough. Just knowing she's safe." He slumped into his chair.

CHAPTER FOURTEEN

Fresh Meat

Bri stared in disbelief at the outside of the building painted a garish purple. The flashing neon sign over the heavy metal door read, "Big Daddy's Topless Bar: 101 Beautiful Dancing Girls and Five Ugly Ones." Her breath caught in her throat. *Have I stooped so low as to be looking for work in a place like this?* she wondered. She again checked the address on the napkin. The number matched. This is where Dana had directed her.

The door swung open. Loud, raucous music burst out into the street. Two men, too inebriated to walk straight, staggered out into the late afternoon sun. A giant of a man whom Bri assumed to be the club's bouncer called to the men. "Go on. Sober up before you come back tonight." The bouncer cast a hungry eye on Bri.

"Can I help you, missy?"

Suddenly tongue-tied, she mumbled, "Is Dana here? I'm here to see Dana."

"She's workin', but her set will be done soon. Come on in and make yourself comfortable. I bet you're the chick Dana told the boss about after she was released from jail this morning. Dumb broad! Getting picked up for fighting in public with old Maisie." Bri almost turned around and ran when the man hungrily licked his lips. "When she called you fresh meat, she meant it."

He clamped his giant fist about her arm and led her into the smoke-filled room. With the room dark, except for the flashing lights on stage and glittering disco balls rotating on the ceiling, it took several seconds for Bri's eyes to adjust, but not before her beefy escort plunked her down at an empty table.

On stage, two women in skimpy attire gyrated on brass poles while a third, the center attraction, moved suggestively to the blaring music as the few customers seated near the stage stuffed dollar bills into her G-string. Bri recognized the woman in the middle as Dana, her cell partner.

The girl's first thought was to flee. This place did not fit into her golden Hollywood dream. She attempted to stand, only to have a man's hand clamp down on her left shoulder.

"Hey, babe, going somewhere?" a strange voice asked. She glanced up at a paunchy, middle-aged man with a cigar dangling from his lips. He wore two of the biggest diamond rings she'd ever seen and several gold chains around his neck.

"Don't run away, little bird. Dana said you might stop by. She said you got into a bit of trouble with the law and would be needing a place to crash for a while." He spoke with a heavy eastern European accent. "So can you dance, or at least smile and move to the rhythm?"

"Uh, yes, I guess so . . . but I don't belong here." Bri glanced both directions, searching for an escape. "Tell Dana thank you for the offer, but I've got to go."

He dropped his rotund body into the nearest chair and let his hand slide down her arm to the back of her hand. "Where you gonna go, sweetheart? From what Dana said, you've burned a whole lot of bridges in the last forty-eight hours."

"Really, I think I should leave." Bri snatched her hand from the man's.

"Now don't be like that. You were working as a party escort and occasional actress, right? By now the escort agency and your acting agency have learned about your arrest and have washed their hands of you. You know that, don't you?"

Startled, she stared into his watery, reptilian eyes. "You don't know that!"

"Oh, baby, trust me. I know how the business works. Every girl in my crib has been where you are right now." He shrugged. "I'm a nice guy. I give them a way of escape until they can get back on their feet and reestablish their careers."

The music on stage rose to a crescendo and stopped to the applause of the small, salivating audience. The three dancers fled off stage as the recorded music shifted to a slower seductive number. A new dancer, wearing kitten ears, a tail, a G-string, and not much else angled her body around the crimson satin curtain one leg at a time. The audience whistled and applauded.

Bri felt sick to her stomach.

"Hey, don't take my word for it. Go back stage and talk to Dana. Tell her Big Daddy sent you." The man at Bri's side moved his chair closer until the smoke from his cigar burned her nostrils. "She'll tell you what a nice guy I am. Hey, Frankie," he called to the 250-pound bouncer, "take this skittish little filly back stage to talk with Dana and the girls."

The bouncer lifted her to her feet and half walked, half carried her toward the curtain at the side of the stage and then down a narrow corridor and into a brightly lit dressing room. Glittery clothing hung on hangers and on every available surface of the room like a circus tent gone mad. Women in various stages of undress sat in front of dressing tables and wall mirrors applying makeup to their faces.

The gaggle of voices instantly ceased as Bri and the bouncer entered. Fear and revulsion swept across the faces of the dancers. "Hey, girls, say Hello to—what did you say your name was? Big Daddy says to make her feel at home."

When Frankie exited the room, the girls turned back to their brightly lit mirrors or to the rack of costumes as if Bri wasn't present, all except Dana. "Come on, kid. Don't be afraid. Frankie's a big old bluff and Big Daddy will be fair with you as long as you treat him nice."

Bri noted an exit sign over a door at the back of the room. "I–I–I think I should leave. Thank you for trying to help me, Dana, but this life isn't for me." When she started toward the door, Bri caught a look of desperation in Dana's eyes.

The woman grabbed Bri's upper arm. "Wait! Where are my manners? How about a cup of coffee and some homemade brownies?" Her wide grin weakened Bri's resolve. The girl relented.

"Fine. Maybe one cup . . . Why not?"

One of the other women grabbed a coffee pot from the hot plate, poured the steaming liquid into a mug, and handed it to Bri. "Thanks."

"Hi, I'm Vera," the girl said. "Do you take it with cream and sugar?"

"No, thank you. I like mine black."

Another woman introduced herself as Libby. She held out a cracked porcelain plate to Bri that was stacked with moist brownies. "Try one. They're yummy."

Uncertain of how to extricate herself from the situation, Bri took the proffered brownie and dipped it into her coffee. "Yum. These are good. Did you make them, Libby?"

"Oh, no. Dana's the chief baker around here. Aren't you, Dana?"

Bri took a second sip of the hot brew and a bite of the brownie. The temperature of the coffee soothed her tired nerves.

Dana smiled and patted the vanity seat. "Here, come sit down, girl. Take a load off." Slowly, Bri did as she was told.

"It's not as bad as it looks. Every girl here has the same dreams as you, and every girl here has run into snags along the way. We're all saving our pennies until we can get back on our feet, so to speak."

One of the girls snorted from behind the rack of costumes. "Back on your feet . . . I like that."

"That's Zelda. Ignore her. She's in a bad mood today. One of her high-tipping regulars chose to spend time with Bridget instead of with her."

"What do you mean, 'spend time'?"

"Well, honey, you make more money when you are *nice* to the customers."

Another snort came from behind the clothes rack.

"Zelda! Stop scaring the girl. Give her time to get her feet wet."

With a hot-pink sequined teddy slung over her arm, Zelda stepped out from behind the clothes rack. Her dyed blond hair trailed strawlike about her shoulders. "Get out while you can, little girl. Your instincts are right! This is no place for the likes of you! Go home to your mommy and daddy while you can." She removed several hair extensions as she spoke.

"Zelda! Zip it!" Dana snarled.

"Oh, are you going to report me to Big Daddy? Go ahead. I don't care. I don't care anymore."

"Ignore her, honey." Dana offered Bri a second brownie. "Which do you like best, the ones with walnuts or without?"

Bri bit into the second piece. "Yum! I think I like the nutty ones."

Dana smiled. "I thought you would."

With each bite, Bri's anxiety lessened until she felt totally relaxed and at home with the strange assortment of dancers. "You look tired, Bri. Why don't you take a short nap while I do my next set?" Dana passed her off to Libby, who led the girl to a small makeshift single bed and mattress behind a purple damask curtain at one side of the room.

"I am feeling quite sleepy," Bri admitted. She handed the empty coffee mug to Libby and curled up on the soft lavender sheet.

Libby covered her with a matching sheet and a zebra-striped afghan. "Sleep well, little girl." The woman's voice sounded sad and distant.

Bri had no idea how long she had slept but when she awoke, the dressing room was abuzz with activity. The evening's show had begun. Thirsty and starving for food, she sat up on the edge of the bed and pulled back the damask curtain. As Zelda rushed by, Bri reached out and touched the woman's bare arm. "Please. I am so hungry. I'm not sure where I am." Her words slurred into soft mush.

"Lie back down and try to sleep it off, honey. Don't worry; Big Daddy will be here for you any minute now."

"Big Daddy?" She licked her parched lips with her tongue. "Who's Big Daddy?"

"Oh, you'll find out soon enough, little girl. Sleep while you can. Just remember, I tried to warn you."

As Bri obeyed the angry young woman, she realized she'd been drugged once again, but this time, with what she suspected to be marijuana. However, she was too sleepy to care. Her limbs felt heavy, yet light as a feather. Again, the voice of her father came to her in a dream. "Honey Bee, I love you. I am praying for you. Come home while you can."

In a half-conscious state, Bri felt someone lift her from the mattress and carry her up a flight of stairs. Her eyes were so heavy, it was easier to relax and go with the flow.

*****

Bri had heard of the human trafficking business but never imagined she'd ever become trapped in it. But she quickly discovered firsthand that it was thriving in L.A. After a few black eyes and bruised ribs, she quickly learned the five house rules as well.

1. Never leave the house without Frankie or one of the bartenders.
2. Never gripe about the conditions or the food.
3. Don't ask a john to help you escape.
4. No substances beyond marijuana and the expected alcohol paid for by a customer.
5. Don't get pregnant.

Breaking any of these rules would earn the miscreant a beating or worse. Bri couldn't imagine what could be worse. When she asked Dana, the woman shuddered and shook her head. "You don't want to know!"

After a few weeks of being at Big Daddy's beck and call, a new girl named Sandi arrived and became his "main squeeze," and Bri was passed on to Frankie, a nightmare worse than the first. On the second floor, the two men had bedroom suites at the top of the stairs. The next four bedrooms accommodated overnight "guests" of the establishment, men who paid for additional favors. That fee was then split 70/30 in Big Daddy's favor.

A dormitory of sorts occupied the rest of the second floor where the dancers lived, if living could describe their conditions. Rows of cots filled the floor space, with a small paint-chipped metal nightstand beside each bed. Bare light bulbs hung down from the ceiling. Small shoulder-high windows let in minimal fresh air and daylight. The dusty panes of glass had been covered with bright citrus-colored silk scarves to "pretty up the joint," as Dana called it, and to block out the early morning sunlight, since mornings were the only time the girls could get an uninterrupted sleep.

From midafternoon until three in the morning, the girls worked, after which they fell into their beds exhausted. One strict rule in the house was that no one opened the drawer of another girl's nightstand. It was there that each girl hoarded what little cash she could save for the day she could break away from the nightmare living situation.

Each night, Bri dreamed the same dream. It was of the face and voice of her father telling her that he was praying for her and he loved her so very much. He would always end the dream with, "Remember, Honey

Bee, I will never leave you nor forsake you." The surreal dream comforted her and gave her the courage to face each new day.

Dana took a personal interest in Bri, teaching her how to execute the most provocative moves on stage and how to most effectively dance around the brass pole. The first time Bri showed up in the dressing room with a black eye, Dana demonstrated how to apply makeup to hide her bruises. "It's important you not miss a night of work," she warned.

One morning Bri awoke minutes before dawn to see Zelda staring out of one of the shoulder-high windows at the industrial alleyway behind the club. Wrapping her frayed sheet about her body, Bri tiptoed to where Zelda stood and touched her arm. The woman started.

"Sorry, I didn't mean to scare you. It's awfully early. What are you doing awake?"

A slight ocean breeze ruffled the woman's tousled hair. "I try to wake up each morning before the others to spend a few minutes praying."

"Praying? In this place?"

"Yes, praying. My mother was, or is, a woman of prayer. It's her faith that keeps me going. Oh, how I want to go home."

"Where is home?" Bri asked.

"A little town outside Davenport, Iowa." Her voice sounded wistful. "From this window, I can see Iowa's clear blue sky; I can smell the corn fields, or as my mama used to say, 'I can hear the corn growin'.' I used to laugh at her naive belief that God answers her prayers, but now it's what keeps me from ending it all." She gave a chuckle. "I think I can hear Mama's corn growin' from this window."

Bri smiled and inhaled the fresh morning air. "My daddy says that at night he can hear the oranges in the orchard growing as well." She paused for a moment. "Did I ever tell you that he grows the sweetest oranges in the valley?"

Zelda wiped a tear from her cheek with the sleeve of her terry cloth bathrobe. "Funny the things you remember when you're gone. What I'd give to spend even one evening rocking on our porch swing with my mother. *Hmm . . .*"

"You wait. Someday you will. I'm sure of it. And someday I'm going to play hide-and-seek in the orange groves with my dad again."

Zelda cast Bri a sad little smile. "You are so innocent. Keep that innocence as long as you can."

Bri opened her mouth to reply, but the sound of Dana stirring on a nearby cot interrupted her thoughts.

"We'd better get back to sleep before all the chatty dancers awaken and another day begins. One word of advice, honey . . ." Her voice dropped to a whisper. "Don't trust Dana. She reports everything to Frankie and he tells Big Daddy."

Bri blinked in surprise. Dana was the last person she'd have suspected of ratting out the girls. The thought brought on a heavy bout of depression.

A bond formed between Zelda and Bri. Two or three mornings a week, they met at the open window and shared their memories of home. One morning, the women declared that they could smell the first blossoms of spring in the air. Zelda confided that she'd finally saved enough cash to buy a bus ticket home. "Please don't tell anyone." Her eyes searched Bri's face. "I can trust you not to tell, can't I?"

"I won't. Of course I won't." Realizing the day would come when she herself would try to flee, Bri asked, "How will you escape? When do you plan on leaving?"

"I can't tell you how because I don't want you to get in trouble for knowing. But when I do, I'll leave immediately after my first set of the evening. That's the time everyone is busy with the most customers. But when I get home to Iowa, I'll let you know I'm safe."

Two nights later, Zelda disappeared after completing her first set for the night just as she'd planned. When the woman missed her second set, Dana asked the dancers if anyone had seen Zelda.

"I think she had a headache and went upstairs for some pain meds," replied Sandi, the girl who'd joined the dancers after Big Daddy and Frankie had found new interests.

Dana took charge. "Sandi, you go find her, and Annie, get dressed to go on for Zelda."

Zelda's bed remained empty throughout the night. When no one mentioned her absence the next morning, Bri secretly cheered for the escapee. For the next week, no one mentioned Zelda by name, but they cast nervous, furtive glances at the empty bed. Bri suspected that each one of them thought the same thing. *Maybe there's hope for me.*

After several days and no message from Zelda, Bri's hopes waned. By this time, rumors circulated through the house that Zelda had left because she was pregnant; that Big Daddy had sold her to an Asian businessman where she was working at his establishment in Hong Kong.

Desperate, Bri turned to prayer. She began slowly mouthing the memorized rhymes of her childhood. "Now I lay me down to sleep . . ." She advanced to the mealtime prayer she'd recited. "God is great; God is good . . ." But she quickly realized it would take more than a childhood poem to rescue her out of her predicament.

The girl recalled how, following her mother's death, when she'd walk into the office, she would find her father seated at his desk, head in hands, begging God for help and strength. She'd heard him beg for wisdom to train Bette in the way she should go and to corral his high-spirited Honey Bee. The idea of praying seemed so alien in this place of horror, almost a desecration of all the good and purity she'd abandoned in her former life. Yet she prayed a simple prayer. "I don't know if You can hear me, but please help me to know what to do to escape this prison."

Awake in the early morning light after dreaming of her father's unchanging message, she'd whisper, "I love you, too, Daddy. Help me. Please help me." If her prayers couldn't work, maybe his could.

One morning, after a tiring night of endless hands pawing at her G-string, she eyed her tasteless breakfast of imitation scrambled eggs, two greasy strips of bacon, and a withered orange. She recalled the lunches of peanut butter and Maude's homemade jam her father's workers ate as they gathered in the orchard during their midday break. She recalled times her dad would surprise the workers with pizza and soda to say thank you for their good work. She recalled how, during the weeks before Thanksgiving, Christmas, and Easter, he'd cater a feast for all his workers and their families. They'd go home with bundles of leftovers, enough to feed their entire families for the next few days. And breakfast, just the thought of Maude's delicious blueberry pancakes made her mouth water.

After Zelda's disappearance, security around the girls became tighter. The dancers were watched round the clock. Bri had just slipped into her Bo Peep costume for her first set when Big Daddy called her into his office behind the bar. Terrified, she wondered if she'd unwittingly done something wrong or if he intended to renew his interest in her. Either would be a nightmare. Trembling, she followed him into the mahogany-lined room. He tossed his key ring onto a peg behind the door, rounded the shiny teak desk, and lowered his bloated body into the overstuffed leather desk chair.

She shuddered at the sight of the cowhide leather sofa where he'd first taken her. From around the room, the stuffed heads of wild animals peered down at her as she paused in the doorway. The glassy eyes of a young fawn looked pleadingly at her, as if begging for life.

"Sit!" Big Daddy ordered. She immediately obeyed. "I'll get right to the point. It seems as though my friend Lim Ki finds you attractive and wants the pleasure of your company while he's in town this week. He just returned from Hong Kong and wants the company of a natural blondie like you. It will be your job to please him in every way you can." She shuddered at the implication. "You will continue to dance each evening as always, but there'll be an extra five hundred dollars for you if he gives you a good report."

Bri took a deep breath and nodded. She immediately recognized Lim Ki's name as the man who'd been spending each evening with Zelda immediately before her friend disappeared. A thought flitted through her mind. *Are the rumors true that Zelda was shanghaied to Hong Kong?*

A knock on the door interrupted Big Daddy's spiel about what a valued customer Lim Ki was. "Come in!" he snapped.

Frankie stepped into the room. He failed to see Bri sitting on the sofa behind the door. "Boss, the cargo's in from Tijuana. What do you want me to do with it?"

Big Daddy eyed Bri as he answered. "Put it in the trunk of my SUV." As Frankie turned to leave, the boss pointed to the heavy key ring on the wall and snarled, "Take the keys, you moron."

"Oh, sorry, boss."

"Go on! Get out of here." Big Daddy pointed toward Bri. "Don't worry about her. She's too smart to run her mouth about what she heard or didn't hear, aren't you, Bri darling?"

"Yes, sir," she nodded as the door slammed behind Frankie.

Big Daddy rose from his chair and lifted her from the sofa by her hands. "Now you go and pretty yourself up for Lim Ki. I'll be sending over my best cognac to guest room number two. He'll be waiting for you after your last set. Don't drink too much, sweetie. Wouldn't want you to pass out on our VIP, would we? Be sure to give him his money's worth."

She exited the office and stumbled back into the din of the strip club. The evening was in full swing. Dana and Libby gyrated on stage to the delight of their drunken fans, while less attractive waitresses replaced their empty glasses with more booze.

Bri hurried to the dressing room. Choosing a purple satin number with a slit up one side to her waist, she weaved hot lavender, pink, and purple hair extensions into her blond curls. She sat down at the makeup tables beside Abby, one of the newer girls, who was gossiping with another dancer. "Well, that's what one of the bartenders told me this afternoon. He said Big Daddy drugged Zelda and shipped her off to Asia. The guy said Big Daddy sold her to his Asian connection because she couldn't keep her mouth shut. Personally, I think she was pregnant! There's no excuse for any of the girls to get pregnant in this day and age!"

Bri's breath caught in her throat. *Could it be possible?* she wondered. She'd heard the rumors before, but she hadn't allowed herself to believe them. Zelda's possible escape was all that had kept Bri going. Before she could react, Dana and Libby rushed into the dressing room and changed into their costumes for their next set.

Frightened, and praying the story wasn't true, Bri reported what she'd heard to Dana. Dana's eyes misted. She pleaded with the younger woman. "Oh, honey, we hear all sorts of things around here. Forget it! Whether it's true or not, you can't let it affect you or your performance, especially with Lim Ki watching. Who knows? This night could change your life forever."

Throughout her set, Bri thought about Dana's words, "change your life forever . . ." The only change Bri wanted was to return home to her father.

CHAPTER FIFTEEN

Frantic Search

Bob slammed his office door and flipped open his cell phone. "Phone contacts . . . phone contacts," he mumbled.

"Who are you calling, Daddy?" Bette glanced up from a stack of contracts she'd been perusing.

"Uncle Jake, my old army buddy. Owens . . . Owens . . . Owens—there it is." He punched in the number. A pause followed and then the familiar voice of his long-lost friend came on line. "Jake! Good morning!"

"Bob Austin, is that you, you old dog?"

"One and the same. So how goes it with you and Marta? Does she still make the best apple dumplings this side of the Mississippi?"

Bette half listened as her father and his friend talked about the long hot drought in the valley and the incessant rains in the Colorado Rockies where Jake lived.

"Wish you could ship some of that precipitation out our way," Bob admitted. He gave a short laugh, and then switched topics. "So have you thought any more about what I might be able to do regarding my missing younger daughter?" He paused, nodded, grunted, and uttered a few "*ums*" and an occasional "I understand."

"Hey, any ideas you may have I'd be mighty grateful. But remember, she mustn't know I had anything to do with it, *capisce?*" He listened a few more minutes. "Well, if you and that pretty little wife of yours find yourselves out my way, remember, *mi casa es su casa.*" He ended the call.

Bette glanced up from the papers in front of her. "How's Uncle Jake?"

"He's doing fine. I sure do miss him. He's been a good buddy since your mother and I met him and his wife, Marta, on our honeymoon at Hoover Dam."

"Do you think it's a good idea to get him involved with finding Bri? Didn't Bri say she'd disappear if anyone came looking for her?"

"Jake has connections, and if anything, he is discreet. I trust him."

Bette shrugged and tapped her pen on the stack of papers. "I hope so. You know how ornery Bri can be . . ." Her voice trailed off.

Bob slammed his hand on the desk. "I've got to do something." His jaw hardened with determination. "Where did you say Ron is working today?"

"He's supervising the harvesting of the Minneola oranges in the Waverly grove, while Ken is picking up new water piping from the hardware store for the new saplings on the west side of Route 99."

"Thanks!" Bob charged out of the house. Behind him the screen door slammed. He dashed across the driveway and climbed into his late model 4 x 4 midnight-blue Silverado. He turned the key in the ignition and the engine roared to life, stirring up a cloud of dust in its wake.

As he directed the truck toward the Waverly grove, his fingers tapped out a message of irritation and worry on the steering wheel. He barely slowed for the turn into the orchard, sending billows of sand and dust into the air, totally obliterating the world behind him. A few feet from the nearest stack of empty pallets, he screeched to a halt and hopped out of the cab. The nearest workers glanced up from their work in surprise.

"Ron Chaney! Where is Mr. Chaney, your supervisor?" he shouted. Taken aback by the big boss's impatient tone of voice, Joe, the nearest migrant worker to him, pointed down a row of orange trees.

"*Gracias!*" Bob shouted. Without glancing at the condition of the orange crop or the trimmed trees, he broke into a trot calling Ron's name as he ran. Looking startled, Ron stepped out from between two rows of trees.

"Yes, sir?"

"Ron, come with me. We need to go over every detail surrounding your and Bri's life at the beach house. There has to be a clue somewhere as to where she could have gone!" Expecting instant obedience, he set a fast pace back toward the truck. As he passed an older worker, Bob called, "Miguel, you take over supervising the team today. Ron needs to come with me."

"Yes, sir." The startled worker scratched his head. Nothing like this had ever happened in the more than ten years he'd worked for 3 B's Orchards.

The boss called over his shoulder. "Mighty hot out here today. Remember to have the workers take regular water breaks."

The two men hopped into the truck. The engine roared to life almost before Ron could close the passenger side door. With one hand, he held on to what the workers called "the glory handle" above the door and with the other, the back of the seat as the vehicle bounced over the ruts and ridges at an unusually fast pace. More than slightly afraid, Ron asked in a staccato voice, "Sir, what's happened? Did someone get injured? Is my mother OK?"

"No accidents! Your mother's fine. I just have a plan to locate Bri and I need your help. I need to know she's safe, regardless of whatever she's choosing to do with her life." Before Ron could answer, he continued. "That's where you come in. I want you to contact your landlady and have her write out every detail of Bri's movements since my daughter turned to her for help. Maybe the woman forgot some detail that could help us locate her. Go back to L.A. if necessary."

"I don't mind doing as you ask, sir, but Bri made it clear she didn't want any of us looking for her," Ron argued. "She's a very stubborn girl."

"I know! I know my daughter, but I can't sit by not knowing if . . ." His voice trailed off as the truck screeched to a stop in front of the Austin home. "Here!" He handed Ron the keys to his vehicle. "Take care. This baby can get away from you at high speeds."

"Your Silverado?" Everyone knew how much Bob loved and babied his 4 x 4.

"I treasure my Honey Bee more, I assure you."

CHAPTER SIXTEEN

Cheap Enough

Ear-shattering music blared through the speakers. The crowd of half-drunken men cheered and waved twenty-dollar bills at the dancers, all except one middle-aged gentleman with graying hair at the temples, muscular shoulders, and arms bulging beneath his polo shirt. He sat off to one side of the stage. Bri had noticed him every night for about a week, nursing one drink and attentively watching the women on stage.

Occasionally, he would call a waitress to his table and point to one of the dancers. The waitress would notify the chosen dancer that the man wished to buy her a drink. Since selling as much booze as possible was one of Big Daddy's main desires each evening, the dancer would sashay over to the man's table and share a drink, being careful to only sip at the alcohol so as to maintain her wits about her. After a few minutes, the girl would leave the table with a large tip stuffed in her G-string, sometimes as much as a hundred dollars. Up to this point, Bri had not been beckoned to his table.

A hundred dollars is a hundred dollars, she mused, casting the man a beguiling smile. Her current benefactor, Lim Ki, had announced the previous night that he would be returning to China at the end of the week. He had begged her to come with him. He had vowed to set her up in her own luxury condo in the best part of the Asian city. So far, she'd held him off with a wave of her hand and a demure smile. But she knew her little diversions would probably not work much longer.

She glanced toward her right at the man about whom all the dancers were gossiping. His expressionless demeanor intrigued her.

Who is this guy, anyway? Bri asked herself as she whirled her lithe, streamlined body around the brass pole for the last spin of her second set for the evening. When she came to a stop, a slobbering drunk with a twenty-dollar bill in his hand pawed at her. She giggled and patted the drunk's unshaven cheek, grabbed the money, and slipped out of his reach just as he lunged toward her. She'd barely recovered her balance on her seven-inch heels when a waitress named Irene whispered in her ear. "The gentleman at table four wishes to buy you a drink."

Finally, it was her turn. She'd begun to think the man preferred brunettes and redheads to blondes. Flipping a long golden curl behind her left ear and pulling her hair on the right side over one eye, she glided to the table with the smoothness and grace of a high-fashion model.

"Hi," she cooed, leaning her upper body into the face of the stranger. "My name is Missy. What can I do for you, honey?" Big Daddy didn't allow any of his dancers or waitresses to reveal their real names to a customer. Even Lim Ki didn't know her name was Brianna.

Unperturbed by her aggressive, yet kittenish manner, the man gestured toward the empty spot on the padded bench beside him. "Please sit. What are you drinking, Missy?"

She eased her seminaked body onto the seat, slid one spike-sandal off her left foot, and lifted her leg into his lap. "*Ooh,* it feels so good to sit for a while. Dancing in seven-inch heels is a killer, I assure you." Her practiced laugh had the ring of a fifteen-year-old's giggle.

Irene, the waitress serving the man's table, appeared at his side. "May I refresh your drink, sir?"

"Yes, I'll take another bourbon and bring a second one for my friend Missy. You do like bourbon, don't you?"

Bri batted her eyelashes and shrugged. "Honey, if you're buying, I'm drinking."

"So," the stranger began, "how long have you been dancing at Big Daddy's club?"

"About a year or so." She ran her foot down the man's thigh and calf. "Been in these parts long, sailor?"

The man blinked in surprise. "How did you know I was in the navy?"

"The anchor tattoo on your right arm is a dead give-away. I used to know a guy with one just like it."

"Really? Are you from around here?"

"I am now," she teased. "Have you been here before?"

"I knew a girl named Zelda. She worked here several months ago. Is she still here?"

Bri froze. *Who is this guy?* She took a deep breath before she replied. "Zelda left soon after I arrived. She returned to her home somewhere in the Midwest, I believe."

Irene arrived with the two drinks and set them on the table. The man slapped a twenty on her tray and turned back to Bri.

Bri lifted her glass toward the stranger. "Cheers."

He did the same. She sipped her drink and ran her tongue over her upper lip. "But enough about Zelda. You haven't told me your name. I'd like to learn all about you. I like your sexy British accent." She'd discovered the best way to divert a man's attention away from unwanted advances and maintain control of the exchange was to coax him to talk about himself.

"Call me Mac. I'm originally from the UK, but haven't been back for quite some time."

"*Ooh,* I'd love to visit England, especially Stratford-on-Avon. 'To be or not to be; that is the question . . .' " She gestured as if she were acting on a Shakespearean stage.

The man gave her a short applause. "Very good. I see we have here a budding actress."

Bri shrugged and sighed, "Once maybe, but now, who knows?"

A new group of dancers gyrated onto the stage, catching his attention for a moment. "Uh, what was that you said?"

"Oh, nothing . . ." She glanced at the man's glass and then ran her forefinger suggestively around the rim of her own. "Would you like Irene to freshen your drink?"

"No, thanks. Tell me, who is that Asian man seated at the bar? He seems to be glaring at us."

Bri laughed and moved closer to Mac, hoping to discourage Lim Ki's interest. "He's harmless. He's got it in his head that I should go with him to Hong Kong as his mistress. He's leaving for China in the morning."

Mac's eyes narrowed. He swirled the amber-colored liquid in his glass. "How do you feel about that?"

"Sheesh! I'm not going with him, I assure you."

He turned and stared into her eyes. "And if he insists?"

The music overrode her confident giggle. "Oh, I can handle him. Lim Ki is a pussy cat."

Bri watched as Lim Ki stood, dropped a bill on the bar, and strode toward Big Daddy's office. His demeanor screamed of anger and determination. She turned back toward her Englishman. "Sorry, but I must go backstage to dress . . ." She blushed. "Or perhaps you might say undress for my third set of the evening."

"Sure. Go ahead, Missy." He stuffed a hundred-dollar bill in her bra strap. "Nice talking with you. It's nice to meet a lovely lady who can quote the Bard. Maybe we can do this again sometime?"

"I'd like that." She was surprised that she actually meant what she said. She slipped her foot into the spike-heel shoe, straightened her skimpy outfit as best she could, and stood. "Thanks for the drink, Mac."

"You hardly touched it," he noted.

"You caught me." She laughed. "Kind of difficult to swing around that brass pole when you're tipsy. See ya later."

With a few minutes to spare, she wriggled into her next costume. She could feel a thunderous headache coming on. Running up the stairs to the rooms, she found a couple of unidentified pills Dana had given her for her last headache.

She swallowed them, took a sip of water, and headed back down the stairs to the dressing room. The door to Big Daddy's office stood ajar. Inside the room, she heard her name being mentioned in an argument between Big Daddy and the voice she knew to be Lim Ki. She paused to listen.

"I want to take her back with me to Hong Kong," the unusually excited man declared. "I've paid you well for Missy's services. After the last fiasco with that Zelda girl, I demand you release her to me. She will add the class I need to my place. How much do you want? A thousand, two thousand, five thousand?"

Big Daddy answered in smooth calculating tones, the man in control of the negotiations. "As you know, Missy is a preferred dancer among my regular customers. She's worth a mighty mint to my business. Did you see that guy tonight drooling over her?"

An edge filled Lim Ki's voice. "How about I throw in a kilo or two of crack? Once my boss sees her, he'll recognize her value."

Bri's breath caught in her throat. *Boss? Lim Ki wants to sell me to his boss? For cash and drugs?* The girl had heard about the active drug trade going on each evening in the topless club. But, except for an occasional joint to steady the nerves, the girls didn't indulge. If Big Daddy caught one of the girls doing so, he'd sic Frankie on her and she'd return to the rooms in the morning with black eyes and bruises that could keep her off stage for a week. A second offense and she'd disappear no one knew where.

Hearing Frankie come up the stairs, Bri dashed down the hall to her room, where she stayed until the three men left. The other girls in her set had already entered the stage when she slipped in as if her late arrival was part of the provocative performance.

"Bri, just where've you been?" Dana hissed as the two other girls massaged the same pole.

"Long story. Tell you later." Bri broadened her smile and swung her body to the second pole, arching back until her long blond curls dragged on the shiny stage floor.

Instinctively, she searched the audience for Mac, but he'd left for the night. Her gaze traveled from man to leering man, desperate to find a sympathetic face in the crowd. She found none. Toward the end of her performance, she saw Big Daddy and Lim Ki exit the office and shake hands. By the grins on their faces, she could tell they'd come to some sort of agreement.

Oh God, the God of my father, she prayed as she swung around the pole to the music. For a moment, she wondered how many dancers had ever prayed while twirling on this stage.

Since meeting up with Big Daddy, Bri couldn't use the word *daddy* when referring to her own father. The girl maintained her own winsome smile for the audience as she danced. *I don't know what to do! I'm so scared! If Lim Ki gets his way, I'll never see my home again.*

A terrifying flash burst out of the blinding lights over her head, the kind you see in horror movies followed by a deafening thunderclap.

Terrified, she shot a glance toward her dancing partners. They hadn't lost a beat. The men in the audience continued shouting and clapping as if nothing had happened. Bri wondered if she'd imagined it and would have continued to wonder until she heard a deafening voice in her ear. *"Brianna, you need to run! This is your one and only chance to escape!"*

Her ears rang. Startled, she glanced around her, certain that everyone in the room had heard the same booming voice. But no one seemed to notice. The dancers continued dancing, the musicians played, the patrons cheered and drank. Big Daddy and Lim Ki stood at the bar laughing like two old drinking buddies. In the rear of the club, she saw Frankie strong-arming a drunken man out the side door into the alleyway. As the door swung open, she could see Big Daddy's shiny black Cadillac SUV glistening under the streetlight.

Bri gyrated her body around the pole, stretched into a back bend, straightened, and dashed off stage beyond the crimson velvet curtains. She grabbed the first available clothing, a red satin robe that came to her thighs, slipped out of the spike-heels and into a pair of Dana's discarded flip-flops.

OK, smarty, she scolded herself, *what now? You have no car, no money, and no one to help you.* Then she remembered Big Daddy's SUV parked behind the club. *I wish I knew how to hot-wire a car!* Then she remembered the key ring inside his office door. Unfortunately, the most direct route to the SUV and the keys involved weaving her way through the crowded club straight past Big Daddy and Lim Ki. Her heart sank.

Dear God, I can't do this alone. I'm so scared! If they catch me, I don't know what they'll do to me.

CHAPTER SEVENTEEN

Alone in the Night

So many nights Bob had paced the hardwood floor of his second-story bedroom, agonizing over and praying for his errant daughter. A late-night e-mail from his friend in Colorado had sent him to the edge of despair. "Sorry, old friend. My L.A. contact is on assignment in San Francisco right now. Don't lose heart. I'll try to get through to him tomorrow."

The clock in the hall gonged twelve before Bob stepped out of the shower where he'd washed away a fresh flood of tears. Compared to most nights since Bri had left home, midnight seemed early. His heart ached as he climbed into his bed and turned out the light. Exhausted, he closed his eyes and willed himself to sleep. "Without the nightmares, dear Lord," he prayed. "Without the nightmares."

"Thou wilt keep me in perfect peace . . ." he quoted. "Keep my mind stayed on You tonight, heavenly Father."

Around three o'clock in the morning, he awoke with a start. He sat straight up in bed. Had he heard a noise outside in the yard? Had a dog barked? He wasn't sure. He rubbed his eyes. Asleep on the foot of his bed, Hiram the cat moaned and moved to the other side of the mattress.

"Pray for Brianna!" a voice ordered. *"Pray for Brianna now!"*

Fighting the temptation to lie back down and return to his dreamless slumber, he dropped to his knees beside the bed.

"Oh, dear God, did You awaken me to tell me to pray for my little girl? OK, I'm doing so. What can I say that I haven't said so many times over the last year or so?" He took a deep breath. "Wherever she is, be with her right now. Give her wisdom and strength. Protect her from whatever evil is about to befall her. You promised in Acts 16:31, 'Believe in the Lord Jesus, and you will be saved—you and your household.' This promise includes my precious Honey Bee. I am counting on You to keep Your word."

Feeling overwhelmingly thirsty, Bob arose and padded his way to the bathroom for a drink of water. As he passed Bri's bedroom door, he felt impressed to go into Bri's room, where he knelt by her bed and claimed the promise a second time.

Light from the moon filtered in from outside as he carried out what he believed to be divine instructions. After she'd left, he had avoided the room—too lonely for him. He preferred to imagine she was at summer camp or attending a slumber party, anything but facing the emptiness of what had become a reality.

Again he knelt and prayed. Again he quoted the verse asking for protection for his younger daughter. As he rose to his feet, his knee bumped against a shoe, Bri's well-worn sneaker. Uncontrolled tears fell. He sat down on the floor and leaned his head against the edge of the mattress. "Help me, Lord." He'd barely uttered the words when a profound peace washed over him, a peace like he hadn't felt in months. As awake as he'd been feeling, he now felt incredibly sleepy. He crossed the hall to the bathroom, got a second drink of water, and returned to his own bed.

He pulled the covers over his body and yawned. Sleepy beyond words, he closed his eyes. And like a royal wand passing over his bed, the troubles of his day faded into the shadows of the night.

CHAPTER EIGHTEEN

Flight of the Honey Bee

Bri slipped back behind the curtain. Inside the dressing room, several of the girls looked up in surprise. "What are you doing here? Aren't you supposed to be on stage?" Sandi asked.

Bri bent down and rubbed her ankle. "I turned it. I think it's swelling."

"Big Daddy won't like that!" Abby applied a fresh layer of mascara to her lashes.

Sandi agreed. "If I were you, I'd slip into those spiky things and at least go out there and mingle with the guests. Maybe he'll understand."

"Yeah, right!" Abby snorted. "He'd only understand if he had to squeeze his big feet into a pair of seven-inch heels and strut around half-naked for an hour or two!"

"*Ooh*, someone's feeling feisty tonight." Bri laughed. "But you're right. Maybe it will help if I schmooze a little. What shall I wear?"

Again Abby snorted. "As little as possible."

Bri slipped out of her outfit and grabbed an emerald green teddy from the rack. "This will do. Now where did those matching heels go?"

Sandi gestured toward the stairs. "I saw them upstairs a few minutes ago."

"Thanks!" Bri ran up the stairs to the rooms and located the shoes. She snatched an envelope holding her meager savings from under her mattress. It was empty. Someone had stolen her hard-earned stash!

There was nothing to do but make her way down the stairs to the bar. Pasting on her brightest smile, she entered the club at the end of what was to be her final set for the evening. As she weaved her way between the tables of drunken men, she allowed them to paw her body more than usual. As a result, they stuffed more cash into her costume. A giggle here, a tickle there, and Bri assessed her progress. She glanced about the smoke-filled room. She spotted Big Daddy on the phone and Lim Ki chatting with Ben the bartender. "Frankie? Where's Frankie?" She muttered under her breath. He could ruin everything if he spotted her leaving the club. She dropped into the lap of a surprised customer who appeared too inebriated to appreciate the gesture. As she cooed in the stunned man's ear, she spotted Frankie coming from Big Daddy's office. Hoping not to be seen, she ducked her head and nuzzled the customer's neck as the bouncer passed her table and headed for the public restroom.

Her gaze swept the room one last time as she eased herself off the man's lap, took the proffered fifty-dollar bill from the customer, and hurried to the closed office door. Praying like she'd never prayed before in her life, she turned the knob. It opened. She reached around the doorjamb to the hook on the wall. A smile crossed her lips, the first genuine smile of the evening, as her fingers wrapped around the massive key ring.

Snatching the keys from the hook, she broke two fingernails. Certain she'd be caught, she dashed out the club's rear door to Big Daddy's parked SUV. A tiny red light blinked from the upper corner of the building—a security camera! Realizing someone inside the club was watching her every move, she panicked. Barely able to breathe, she chose what she hoped was the right key, climbed in, and slammed the door behind her. It took both of her quivering hands to direct the key into the ignition.

The engine roared to life. The powerful SUV lunged forward, crashing into and sending a barrage of garbage cans across the alleyway. She cringed at the damage the metal cans might have done to Big Daddy's paint job and then let out a hysterical laugh that ricocheted off the walls of the empty vehicle. "Any damage the cans might have made will be nothing compared to the damage Big Daddy will do to me if he catches me!"

She pressed the gas pedal to the floor and careened onto the main street. Spotting a sign for a northbound entrance to the freeway, she whipped the vehicle past a slower moving car and cut him off. The driver reacted by laying on his horn and gesturing angrily. "Sorry, buddy. You shouldn't be out at this hour anyway!"

Bri pressed her foot against the gas pedal and held it as the car zoomed into the flow of traffic. Weaving in and out between vehicles, she laughed. "Thanks, Dad, for teaching me how to maneuver the potholes in the orchards! As I see it, tonight will end in one of four ways. Either I'll kill myself in a car wreck; I'll get caught by Frankie or someone equally despicable; I'll get arrested for speeding and spend the night in jail; or I'll make it home in a couple of hours."

The last possibility kept her focused during the long drive over to I-5. Every set of headlights she spotted following her forced her to drive faster. With every mile, the traffic grew lighter. She gave a wild war whoop when the lights of the tiny town of Grapevine came into view. As she eased into the first gas station to fill up the tank, a patrol car pulled up beside her. The policeman climbed out, tipped his hat toward her, and strode into the convenience store. Her stomach gurgled. It had been several hours since she had eaten or even used a restroom. Both were urgent at the moment.

As she touched the door handle, the glitter of emerald green sequins reminded her of her state of undress. Panic returned. *I can't traipse inside that store wearing this outfit! I can't even get out of the car to pump any fuel in this getup!* She banged the palm of her hand against the steering wheel and cried, "Now what?"

She glanced at the needle on the dashboard gauge. It registered on empty. She'd have to fill up soon. Knowing she had another two hours of driving ahead of her and that the vehicle drank fuel like some of the club's regulars drank alcohol, she shouted, "You started this, God! You'll have to finish it!"

Realizing she had to risk running out of fuel alongside the highway, she fought to control her nerves. "Slowly! Slowly! Don't draw attention to yourself." Bri pulled away from the pumps and gingerly drove back onto the freeway, carefully checking her rearview mirror for a police car that might have followed her or for Frankie and his thugs who might be chasing her.

Knowing the high speeds she'd been driving would cause the SUV to use more fuel, she slowed to sixty, activated the speed control, and prayed. Between prayers, she checked the gas gauge. The needle hadn't moved. Thinking the needle had gotten stuck, she tapped the glass. It didn't budge. Mile after mile, the needle didn't move as she drove past fields of cotton and corn.

Tears trickled down her cheeks when she exited the freeway and drove the last three miles to her father's home. She rolled into town past Hank's Hardware Store where her father bought his supplies and past Betty's Cafe where she and Ron had shared English muffins and hot chocolate after late-night dates . . . There'd been many times during the last year when she'd wondered if she would ever see the familiar sights of home again. In fact, she hardly thought of the family homestead as her home anymore. She knew she didn't deserve it. She'd tossed everything aside for what she'd hoped would be a life of wealth, fame, and glamour. As she drew closer to the valley, doubts bombarded her mind. *What if he won't take me back? I wouldn't blame him. I don't deserve anything from him. What am I going to say?* The idea of disappearing into the night never to be seen again tempted her. But no, Bri decided that after surviving a life of degradation and slavery, she couldn't end it all by slamming the SUV into a concrete highway abutment.

Once she'd erased that temptation from her mind, she rehearsed her plea to her father to hire her as one of his orchard workers. Even if he rented one of the workers' motel-like rooms to her, she'd have a roof over her head and three adequate meals a day. *All I can do is try,* she reasoned. She glanced down at her broken fingernails and grinned. *You can forget about having perfectly manicured nails working in the orange groves. And you'll have to trade in your satin teddy for a pair of blue jeans and a flannel shirt,* she mused. As she turned the giant SUV onto her father's property, she shouted for the world to hear, "It's fine with me if I never wear another teddy again!"

CHAPTER NINETEEN

An Unexpected Reception

Autumn had arrived in the valley; a chill filled the air. Newly fallen leaves whisked about Maude's feet as she climbed the back steps and crossed the wide veranda to the Austins' kitchen door. Mumbling to herself as she opened the back door, she reviewed her breakfast menu. "I think I'll whip up a Spanish omelet with peppers, mushrooms, onions, and leftover salsa. Mr. Bob loves my Spanish omelets." She hung her hand-knitted woolen sweater on a hook behind the door and slipped into her Mother Hubbard apron. "Home fries will be good with the omelet. I do need to squeeze some fresh oranges for juice."

As the woman washed her hands in the sink, she heard the roar of an unfamiliar vehicle approaching at an incredible speed. She glanced out the window at the black SUV as it whipped around the farmhouse and screeched to a halt behind the house. The driver's side door flew open and a half-naked Brianna leaped from the vehicle and dashed for the kitchen door. The housekeeper's jaw dropped in astonishment. Before Maude could react, Bri flew into the house and rushed past the woman and into the hall bathroom.

"Sorry, Maude. I gotta go!" Both the bathroom door and the kitchen door slammed simultaneously.

Breaking free of her initial astonishment, Maude ran to the foot of the stairs. "Mr. Bob! Get on down here right away! Ya gotta see this!" The unflappable housekeeper's excited voice stirred consternation in Bob Austin as he stepped out of the shower. Fearful something terrible must have happened, he hauled his boxer shorts and blue jeans over his wet body. He grabbed his white terry cloth bathrobe off the foot of the bed, struggling into it as he ran to the top of the stairs. His frightened mind concocted a running series of possible accidents and tragedies. "What happened, Maude? Are you all right?"

"Just get down here right now!" The woman's voice cracked with excitement.

The man took the stairs three at a time. "Whatever happened to set you off like this? Are you all right?"

His foot hit the bottom step as Bri, wearing the briefest swatch of emerald green satin, stepped out of the hall bathroom. "Hi, Daddy . . ." Her frightened voice trailed off in doubt.

Her father froze midstep. Was his mind deceiving him? Was his imagination playing cruel tricks on him? He glanced toward his weeping housekeeper and then at the girl.

"Daddy, I'm so sorry. I didn't know where else to go. I know I don't deserve to be welcomed back as your daughter and I don't deserve your forgiveness." She knew she was babbling as tears flooded her face. "But if you're willing to hire me to work in the orchards for you, I promise I'll work hard. I'll earn every dime of your money. Just give me a chance . . ."

He felt his heart would break. The woman standing before him wasn't the little girl he'd waved goodbye to a little more than a year ago. Her skin looked haggard and sallow. The shine from her natural blond hair had deadened to a faded, strawlike shade of yellow. Rivulets of old makeup stained her cheeks. But it was her eyes that disturbed him the most. Cynicism and pain had replaced the vibrant innocence he remembered.

Before she could finish reciting the speech she'd rehearsed dozens of times on the way up Interstate 99, he reached toward her. "Oh, Honey Bee, you're home. That's what matters."

As he engulfed her in his arms, he realized the girl was quivering. Shedding his robe, he wrapped it around her and drew her into his arms. "*Sh-sh-sh,* little one. Everything's going to be all right."

As he held her, he recalled the times he'd coaxed her as a little child back to sleep after a nightmare; the times he'd bandaged her bruised knee after she fell from the backyard swing; and how in the third grade he'd consoled her aching heart when her crush had rejected her for her best friend Judy.

Struggling to pull herself together, Bri pulled free of his grasp. "No, Daddy, I don't deserve to be called your daughter any longer. I've done terrible things, things so horrible I can't even mention. I've wasted all of Grandpa's trust fund. I've pushed away everyone who ever loved me—you, Ron, everyone. And on top of everything else, I've stolen a nightclub owner and drug dealer's car!" She shook her head and hid her face from his gaze. "I really do mean it! I will gladly harvest oranges, trim trees, or pull weeds if you'll only help me out this one last time."

But her father wasn't listening. "Honey Bee, you're still shivering. Go on up to your room, take a hot shower, and get some rest. You look beat. Are you hungry? I'll have Maude bring you a breakfast tray with all of your favorite foods." He held her face between his two rough and chapped hands. "Your old clothes are there. Everything is just as you left it." To Maude, he added, "I have some calls to make and you have a party to plan!"

"A party?" Maude started in surprise. "When?"

"The sooner the better."

"It should be a big, big south-of-the-border party with piñatas and a mariachi band, and garden lights, and enchiladas, lots of enchiladas! Hundreds of tamales too! Hire a dozen women to help you with the preparation. You take care of the food and I'll do the rest. My daughter has come back home! That is reason to celebrate!"

The older woman smiled as she watched a new zest for life enter her boss. "We've got lots to do!" He snatched his cell phone from his pocket. "My daughter was dead to me and now is alive again; she was lost and now is found!" He called each of his friends. When he came to Ron's number, he hesitated. Ron had entered the police academy and was currently dating another girl. *Maybe I shouldn't invite him. No, Ron is a vital piece of Bri's experience. He has been a part of this family for more than a decade and he would want to know.*

He hit the call button before he could change his mind. "Ron? This is Bob Austin. Thought you'd like to know that Bri has come home and I'm throwing her a welcome home party tomorrow evening. It starts at six. Sure would like it if you and your mother could attend."

"Yeah, sure. I'm so glad she's safe. Sir? I know this is awkward, but may I bring Amy Evans with me?"

"Amy? But of course."

"You know Amy and I have been seeing each other for three months or so now."

"Yes. Don't feel guilty for moving on. No matter what the future holds for both of you, you are one of Bri's closest friends and she'd want you to be here celebrating. But I do have a favor to ask of you." Bob told the young man about the stolen SUV and the possible stash of drugs in the back. "I'm sure the Caddie has GPS tracking. So I'm worried that some yahoos are going to show up at any time, looking for trouble. Any ideas how we can get the vehicle back to its owner without bringing on any trouble?"

"You're right about the GPS tracking. One thing you should do is have Ken or someone park it ten miles or so from your home. In the meantime, I'll ask some of my police friends about what we can do and I'll let you know."

Bob placed his final call to Bri's older sister. His excitement burst from him as he told her about her sister's return. Instead of the joy he expected to hear from Bette, silence greeted him.

"Isn't it incredible? I feared I'd never again see her alive."

A long pause followed. "Of course I'm glad she's safe. But why throw a party? Hasn't she brought enough shame to this family without rubbing our friends' and neighbors' noses in it? You do know what she's been doing for the last year, don't you?"

"Yes, I do, but that's not the point. She's home now! It's time to surround her with our love."

"Huh! Of course Ken and I will be there to honor the family name, but as for the rest—haven't we always?"

"What is wrong with you? I don't understand."

A distinct pout flooded her voice. "When was the last time you threw a party for me, Daddy? Do Ken and I get a party for all the years we've worked by your side, kept your books, and run your crews?"

Bob scratched his head. His brow furrowed. "Are you afraid I'll split your share of the business with her? You don't need to worry. Financially, nothing's changed. Everything I have is yours."

Bette mumbled a few unintelligible words, and then hung up. His heart heavy with sadness, Bob pushed through his pain to call the town's best event coordinator, asking her to handle the rest of the details. He'd barely hung up when Ron called.

"Hi, Mr. B. I discussed Bri's situation with a few of my buddies at the police academy. They agree that the first thing you need to do is get that SUV off your property as quickly as possible. If the GPS is working—and there's no reason to believe it isn't—you are in real danger."

"I agree. I've asked Ken to help me move it. We thought we'd drive it to the interstate rest stop north of town."

"Good idea. Just wanted to tell you that the guys and I have come up with a plan, but it could be risky. Do you have time this morning for a sit-down before we try to pull it off?"

"Sure, where shall we meet? At Rosa's Waffle House?"

"Sounds good. I'll be there in fifteen minutes."

*****

The meeting at Rosa's Waffle House lasted throughout the afternoon. All parties agreed that the Cadillac could put the Austins in serious danger, but after that point, they differed.

"What I don't understand is why he hasn't already called it in as stolen," Joe, a rookie officer with the town police department, said.

"Probably because he'd rather not have the authorities poking around his own nefarious business activities," Ron reasoned. "By the way, Mr. Austin, did you remove any fingerprints in the vehicle that could be traced back to you or to Bri?"

"Yes, Ken and I wiped down the seat, dashboard, keys, and steering wheel with hand sanitizer after we parked it at the rest stop. I purposely left the doors unlocked and the key ring in the ignition, hoping someone would come along and heist the car."

The men laughed.

"Good work, Mr. Austin. That would serve the scoundrels right!" Rupert, a burly six-foot-five, first-year cadet at the police academy chortled. "Only fair if you ask me."

"We can't risk leaving it parked at the rest stop and having an astute CHP officer find it and call it in," Bob added.

Joe frowned. "But we can't overlook the fact that by our knowing the vehicle is stolen and doing nothing about it, we are open to possible prosecution should something happen that we didn't expect."

"Just by knowing about the theft we're already accessories after the fact," Steve, another of the seven police friends Ron had recruited reminded them.

"But somehow, we gotta get these guys!" Ron pounded his fist on the table. "Look what they're doing to the lives of so many young women."

"Perhaps you're too close to this, Ron. Maybe you need to back off and let me drive the vehicle down to L.A." The older and wiser Bob shook his head. "I don't want any of you guys to get into trouble or worse yet, get hurt, dealing with these thugs."

Ron tapped his fork on the red marbled Formica tabletop. "No, sir, I disagree. You're too close to the situation. I still think the best idea is my first one." He went on to explain. "If, by tomorrow night, the SUV is still parked at the rest stop, I'll drive it to L.A. The rest of you guys can follow in Rupert's father's Ford Excursion, so that I have a ride home. That way, if the law gets involved, I will be the only one of us who actually touched the Caddie. The rest of you will technically be in the clear. I will tell Big Daddy and his goons to stay away from Bri in exchange for the vehicle. For him to try to find her would have diminishing returns, especially if we tell him the California Highway Patrol will be watching for him or his buddies if he drives one mile beyond the Grapevine."

"And you think he'll hesitate to take you out on the spot?" Rupert shook his head and scratched his face. "The only threat his kind will understand is force. All of us will need to back you to make it work."

"I don't know. I see so many holes in your plan, Ron," Bob argued. "For instance, what if the thugs decide to challenge you?"

Ron shrugged. "It's OK, Mr. B. We have until tomorrow night to work out the kinks, right? And we will, I assure you. No one is going off half-cocked."

Rupert added, "We won't leave until after the party, right?"

*****

While the idea of a party didn't thrill Bri, she reluctantly agreed to go along with her father's plans. She could only imagine how embarrassing it would be facing all their friends after what had happened to her.

"I left home a star and returned a tramp!" she moaned.

"You are still my daughter and I will never think of you as a tramp. Never! You got caught up in an evil you never even imagined existed." Bob had almost always relented to Bri's wishes. This time he remained calm but insistent.

"You don't know how much they'll gossip about me behind my back."

"That will happen regardless, but by facing it head-on, you can honestly answer their questions and defuse their ammunition. Sooner or later, you have to face what happened. You don't want to become an old maid hermit held up in some mountain cabin for the rest of your life, do you?"

Her eyes were round with trepidation.

He continued. "Eventually, you will have to deal with your past and when that happens, having the strong and loving support of your family and community will make it much easier."

"But what do I say, especially to Ron and his mother?"

"You thank them for attending the party and for their friendship during this rough time. If you feel the need to apologize, then apologize for the pain you've caused them." Bob's brow furrowed. He leaned forward and took her two hands in his. "You need to know that Ron has moved on. He is seriously dating a girl named Amy. I think she was a couple of years behind you in school. Amy will be at the party."

Tears glistened in Bri's eyes. "Oh, Daddy, no, I can't do this."

"Yes, you can. Think of the party as your final acting performance before a friendly audience. The guests are my friends, too, you know. If they reject you, they are rejecting me as well." He wiped away a tear streaking down the side of her right cheek. "Bri, you have been through a lot and, whether you know it or not, you are stronger because of it. I can see a new determination in your eyes. If you don't face your demons, Big Daddy and his kind will win. They will destroy you. You are too stubborn to let that happen. I have faith in you, little one. You're one tough little Honey Bee."

Bri smiled at his use of her pet name. Coming from his lips, it almost made the young woman believe his words. "And what about the SUV? I stole it!"

Bob waved a dismissive hand in the air. "Don't worry about that little detail. You did what you had to do to escape. Ron, a bunch of his buddies, and I have that detail covered. The less you know, the better. In the meantime, take a shower, style your hair, put on your prettiest dress, and prepare to celebrate in the best Austin manner."

Bri took her father's advice. Even though the majority of friends and neighbors were attending out of respect for him, she determined to put on her best face, answer all questions, and demonstrate to the world that she was indeed an Austin.

CHAPTER TWENTY

The Midnight Caper

When the clock in the Austins' hallway struck ten, Bob stole away from the festivities. Ron, looking dashing in his policeman's uniform, kissed his mother and Amy goodbye. He and seven other men also dressed in their rookie uniforms slipped into the office where Bob waited. "Before you go," Bob took a deep breath, his eyes worn and tired, "we need to ask God for protection."

The solemn-faced men nodded and bowed their heads.

"Dear heavenly Father, it's been a long struggle getting to this point. Events have happened that none of us could have foreseen. You know our motives are pure and our hearts are clean. You also know this venture could turn dangerous. Intervene in whatever way necessary to protect these young men. Bring them home safely. In Your Son's holy name. Amen."

Bob again made a final plea to go with them. "Bri is my daughter. I have a responsibility to go."

"No!" Ron stood with his thumbs in his belt laden with the tools of his trade. "Bri needs you here. If this caper, as you call it, goes south, you wouldn't want to leave her unprotected, would you?"

Bob heaved a sigh. "I guess not."

"For that matter, we've been talking." Ron exchanged glances with the other men. "After your guests leave, why don't you take her to the coast for the next few days? A break would do you both good; maybe take Ken and Bette along—time to begin healing, you know?"

Bob understood the reasoning behind Ron's suggestion. "What you say makes sense. If we're not in the area, Big Daddy can't hunt us down. Besides, maybe someone has already stolen the Caddie and all of our planning is in vain." He could tell by the looks on the men's faces that they hoped a theft had not occurred. They were men eager to carry out their mission. The group exchanged handshakes with Bob while Ron grabbed a giant cooler of sodas, egg salad sandwiches, and chocolate chip cookies that Maude had prepared for them, and a second smaller cooler containing goodies to carry in his vehicle.

"See you in the morning." Ron gently punched Bob's arm.

At the rest stop, the men discovered that the Cadillac SUV had not been disturbed. Ron laughed as he climbed out of his friend's SUV and opened the door of the other. "Keys are still in the ignition," he called to his waiting friends. "Life isn't fair. Just when you'd appreciate having some scoundrel heist a vehicle, people become honest!"

The seven other men laughed.

"See you in L.A." He climbed into the Cadillac, started the engine, and tooted the horn as he headed south on the interstate.

Several shooting stars streaked across the clear night sky making the drive south almost magical. The men had agreed to make a fuel stop at the base of the Grapevine. They would avoid drawing attention to their two-vehicle caravan by not conversing with one another.

Flipping through the stations on the radio, Ron located an all-night FM station broadcasting contemporary Christian music. He decided he could use some reassuring comfort as he drove. He settled back for the long drive over the mountains and into the L.A. basin. When the vehicle climbed the Grapevine, his mind wandered to his and Bri's fateful drive to Hollywood. He grimaced from the pain of what he'd come to think of as the beginning of the end for their romance. His heart ached for what might have been. But like all destructive habits a person develops, he knew he'd taken the necessary time to get over her. Seeing her again hadn't revived his old feelings for her; he only felt pity for all she'd been through.

His mind shifted to happier moments. How different his budding relationship was with Amy. The quiet, unassuming young woman's smile could brighten his heart after a long day of working in the orchards or studying for his finals at the academy. With a picnic basket in the backseat of his Junker, Amy enjoyed long drives in the foothills, which she called "day trips." They would spread out a blanket on the side of the road, eat peanut butter and jelly sandwiches, and toast one another with apple cider in plastic stemware.

Amy dreamed of becoming an elementary school teacher. Ron loved her gentle nature with kids, with animals, and particularly with his mother. But Ron especially adored her spontaneous laughter. Amy could find humor in the strangest of happenings.

Hours later, Ron pulled the SUV into the darkened alleyway behind the club and turned off the engine and headlights. He watched through his rearview mirror as Rupert eased to a stop behind him and doused his lights as well. Except for the blare of raunchy music coming from the club, the night fell unusually silent as if all of nature held its breath anticipating the drama about to unfold. He spotted the blinking red light of the security camera over the exit sign and held his breath. Someone watching from inside the bar would quickly take note of the arrival of the boss's vehicle, or so he thought.

Eyeing the lone exit for any movement, he opened the door on the driver's side, slipped out, and dropped into a crouching position. Behind him, he heard Rupert and his buddies do the same. Mentally preparing for the worst, he inched along the driver's side of the SUV. At any moment, he expected the door to the club to burst open and a gang of hoodlums to emerge with guns drawn. Instantaneously, as he heard a rustle to his left and turned, a massive gloved hand clamped over his mouth. Ron struggled against his attacker's massive bulk but couldn't escape. Behind him, he heard the door to Rupert's car open along with the scuffle of boots and angry whispers.

Great, Ron thought as his attacker pressed his face against the brick wall next to the exit door of the club. *We're caught before we had a chance to do anything. Oh, God, now would be a good time for You to answer Mr. Bob's prayer!*

"*Sh-sh-sh!* Don't make a sound," his opponent growled in his ear. Silently, with great stealth, ten men wearing black sweatshirts and pants under bulletproof vests, with semiautomatic guns drawn, emerged from the shadows and surrounded the occupants and the two cars. Terrified, Ron tensed, waiting for the shower of bullets to begin.

He held the car keys up over his head. "Here are your keys. We brought the SUV back to you." His voice cracked, like that of a young male teen. In response, his attacker pressed Ron's body tighter against the wall until he thought his rib cage would crack.

"FBI. Keep your face to the wall! Put both hands over your head," a gruff voice demanded. Ron did as he was told and the stranger clamped metal handcuffs on Ron's wrists. By the sound of it, his friends were experiencing the same treatment. The agent patted Ron down and then removed Ron's wallet and cell phone from his pockets.

The man whipped Ron around and shined a flashlight in his eyes. "Who are you? What are you doing here?" The man glanced down at Ron's clothing. "You're a cop? You're all cops?"

Ron reddened. "Yes and no. Sir, I can explain—"

"I'm sure you can. So why were you driving Hector Rodman's SUV?"

"Hector who?" Ron averted his eyes from the blinding light.

"Don't try to deny it. We followed you blokes for several blocks."

Ron gulped. "Blokes? My name is Ron Chaney. My friends and I are returning this vehicle to its rightful owner, Big Daddy." Ron paused and blinked. "His name is Hector?"

"Whoa! Slow down." The man spoke with a distinctly British accent. The man waved to his companions. "Load them into our vehicles for safekeeping while we get the truth out of these guys."

"You do know we're under surveillance from inside the club. Big Daddy, er Hector, and his men could charge out of that door at any moment," Ron warned.

The head agent snorted, "Not likely. We have a man on the inside taking care of that possibility." He turned to the other agents. "Dustin, Isaac, you search their SUVs. Brad and Mike, stand guard at the exit in case someone comes out. OK, let's hear your story."

Except for the men crouched behind garbage cans on each side of the club's exit, the alleyway grew strangely empty and silent. The head agent's face remained hidden in the shadows while Ron told the story of Bri having worked at that club and of her escape.

"Captain." The man referred to as Isaac tapped on the driver's window. "We found crack in the Cadillac's wheel well, lots of crack."

The agent shined the flashlight in Ron's eyes. "Drugs! And I almost believed your blarney!"

"Please believe me, sir. None of us knew there were drugs in that SUV. We just wanted to get the vehicle to its proper owner and head home as quickly as possible."

"While wearing uniforms?"

"Obviously that was a mistake. We thought Big Daddy and his men would be less likely to attack us if we wore our uniforms. We are police officers, sir, at least, police cadets."

Swallowing a grin, the agent shook his head. "You guys almost messed up an international bust for human trafficking. Fortunately, your friend's story matches with the one a woman named Zelda told the American embassy officials in Hong Kong. Uncuff him, Bruno."

"Yes, Captain." The officer named Bruno removed the handcuffs. Ron rubbed his wrists to reestablish circulation in his hands and fingers.

"Sorry for the cuffs, son. Call me Mac. We've been watching Hector Rodman's place for weeks. The FBI got a lead from Hong Kong where a young woman escaped from a brothel to the embassy, where she told the officials about originally being trafficked out of this establishment and later, being shanghaied to China."

"The poor woman," Ron breathed. "You say you've staked out the place for a few weeks. Then you might have seen my friend Bri, dancing in there, a blonde, barely twenty?"

Mac grinned. "Sure did; charming girl, definitely too classy for such an establishment. She quoted Shakespeare to me. But she told me her moniker was Missy." Mac's stoic demeanor quickly returned. "Finding those drugs in the wheel well and the arrest for human trafficking should put these idiots behind bars for several years."

"Good. Whatever their sentences are, they can't be long enough for me!" Ron's eyes flashed with anger and then grew tender. "Tell me, what will happen to Zelda? Bri will want to know. They became friends during the time they were here."

Mac nodded. "You know I shouldn't be telling you any of this. Oh, well, I've already said too much. Zelda has agreed to become a state's witness, both here in the U.S. and for the Chinese government. When she arrives stateside, she will be taken into the witness protection program until it is deemed safe for her to return to her family. Currently, she is in protective custody at the American Embassy."

"Thank you, sir. Bri will be so glad to hear that. But what about her, will she need to testify as well?"

"We'll try to keep her out of it, but if the other girls refuse to help us, we may need her to convict these miscreants. We can find her if we need her." Mac spoke into the radio attached to his shirt collar. "OK, boys, let them go. They have a long drive home."

"How do you know where to find Bri?"

Mac cast Ron a wry grin. "You'd be surprised at all we know, Mr. Chaney. Give my regards to your mother."

"My mother?"

Mac climbed out of his vehicle and shook hands with Ron.

"It was, I can't say nice, but an adventure, meeting you, Captain. You sure you don't need our help subduing those guys?" Ron cocked his head to one side and grinned up into Mac's face.

Mac broke into a smile. "I think we can handle it from here. Now you guys better disappear before I change my mind and arrest you for possession of a stolen vehicle."

"Yes, sir!" Ron snapped off a smart salute and dashed toward Rupert's father's SUV. "I get to ride shotgun," he hissed in a stage whisper to his friends.

Epilogue

At the beginning of this book, I asked where a story like Brianna's begins. Now, as I write the last pages of her tale, I wonder where Bri's story ends. Jeremiah 29:11 says, "I know the plans I have for you."

Ron and Amy married the following summer. Bri looked lovely in lavender silk as one of Amy's bridesmaids. Currently, the couple resides in Northern California where Ron walks the beat as a rookie police officer and Amy teaches twenty-five wriggly first-graders.

As for Brianna, she has learned that choices have consequences. The lessons have been painful, and her recovery slow. But as old dreams dissolve into cold reality, new goals emerge out of life's tragedy. Bri is studying to become a social worker. Her heart's desire is to help other women regain their lives after escaping from human trafficking.

While Bette and Ken still work for the family business, her main devotion has shifted from 3 B's Orchards to the arrival of her own little B—Bobby IV. And Grandpa couldn't be happier.

enditnow®

Break the Silence About Abuse

"To heal the brokenhearted, to proclaim liberty to the captives . . . to set at liberty those who are oppressed." —Luke 4:18, NKJV

*A*buse of any kind, whether perpetrated against women, men, girls, or boys, is evil. Besides gender, abuse crosses all cultural, racial, socioeconomic, and religious or denominational boundaries. If you sense someone is facing abuse, offer empathetic help and hope. If you are the victim, seek help. *You are not alone.*

While it is true that abuse occurs within every demographic, violence against women is pandemic. The United Nations estimates that, globally, at least one in three women experiences physical and/or sexual violence in her lifetime.

Among women aged 15–44, acts of violence cause more death and disability than cancer, malaria, traffic accidents, and war combined.

Women and girls constitute 80 percent of the estimated 800,000 people trafficked annually, with the majority (79 percent) trafficked for sexual exploitation.

Human trafficking in the United States:

- Human trafficking generates an annual revenue of *$9.5 billion* in the U.S.
- Approximately *300,000 children* are at risk of being prostituted in the U.S.
- The average age of entry into prostitution for a child victim in the U.S. is 13–14 years old.
- *One in three teens* on the street will be lured toward prostitution within 48 hours of leaving home.

You can stop the violence!

For more information, go to:

www.EndItNowNorthAmerica.org
www.nadwm.org

Women's
MINISTRIES
NORTH AMERICAN DIVISION
of SEVENTH-DAY ADVENTISTS

National Domestic Violence Hotlines
USA: 800-799-SAFE (7233)
Canada: 800-363-9010